GO FIND
DADDY

ALSO BY STEVE GOBLE

ED RUNYON MYSTERIES

City Problems

Wayward Son

SPIDER JOHN MYSTERIES

The Bloody Black Flag

The Devil's Wind

A Bottle of Rum

Pieces of Eight

GO FIND DADDY

AN ED RUNYON MYSTERY

STEVE GOBLE

OCEANVIEW PUBLISHING
SARASOTA, FLORIDA

ISBN 978-1-60809-620-6

Published in the United States of America by Oceanview Publishing

Sarasota, Florida

www.oceanviewpub.com

10 9 8 7 6 5 4 3 2

For my Gere

GO FIND DADDY

CHAPTER ONE

THE TURKEY BUZZARDS found Officer Brandon Gullick before anyone else did.

The ravenous birds and a morning of hard rain had done away with a lot of valuable evidence around Donny Blackmon's barn, where the body was found, but one quite damning thing remained: Blackmon's gun, with a piece of his thumbprint on it.

And now Donny Blackmon's wife was begging me to find the man every cop in the country would love to find—and maybe kill, if they got the chance. Blackmon was a blogger, and he did not like police officers one damned little bit. Now most people seemed to think he'd gone and murdered one.

Law officers take such things personally. I know. My name is Ed Runyon, and I'm a private investigator. I used to be a cop.

"Please, Mr. Runyon," Amy Blackmon implored. "I just want you to find him."

I leaned forward. I was staring at her across a small kitchen table, through the steam from a cup of coffee I hadn't really wanted because of the June heat, but which she had insisted on making anyway. She had a lot on her mind, naturally enough, and being hospitable was sort of her way of dealing with it. It's rural Ohio. A visitor comes, you make coffee. That's what you do.

It felt alien to see her whole face. I'd shown up at her home wearing my COVID-19 mask, a nice one Linda got me that sported the Ohio State football logo. But Amy Blackmon had opened the door and said, "We don't wear those in here." Ohio had recently relaxed its rules, and I had already been fully vaccinated, so I had removed the mask before going inside.

Now, Amy Blackmon was staring at me with blue eyes intent on bending me to her will. Her forehead was creased with worries, and her long blonde hair had been combed hurriedly, if at all. She reminded me a little of the late Carrie Fisher. She had that same attitude: "I'm going to say what I think, and you're just going to have to deal with it."

"Please, call me Ed. Ms. Blackmon, what makes you think I can find your husband? Cops all over the state, hell, all over the country, have been looking for him for three months."

"I go to church with Tammy Zachman," she said. "She tells me you did a hell of a job for her and her boy Jimmy."

"I did OK." Jimmy Zachman had gotten himself caught up in an online sex blackmail scheme and run away from his strict Christian parents because he could not bear the thought of them thinking he was hell-bound for what he'd done. What he'd done was the same thing every other fifteen-year-old boy does, but he'd done it on a video call with someone he thought was a nice gay guy. That, of course, led to blackmail. The frightened boy had fled home and proceeded to run into problems that were way, way worse than a blackmail scheme, and I'd been damned lucky to get Jimmy and his friend—and myself, for that matter—out of it alive.

That had been more than a year ago, and I'd managed to stay out of such scrapes since. My fledgling private investigation business was getting by on a steady diet of two-timing husbands and new-hire background checks. It was all boring, of course, but after a couple of near-death experiences, I was fine with boring.

This Blackmon case was anything but boring.

I was not particularly eager to go looking for a man accused of killing a cop. Especially when that man's blog called cops "the armed thugs of a criminal, illegitimate government." And most especially when there was very little reason at all to think he hadn't shot Officer Brandon Gullick in the head. Twice.

The trail was already frozen cold, too, and the internet buzzed with misinformation. Half of the people on Twitter believed Donny Blackmon to be proven guilty, while the other half had turned him into a folk hero who'd offed a cop on behalf of the oppressed. For every Facebook page urging justice for Officer Gullick, there was another proclaiming Donny Blackmon innocent.

And the sightings, hoo boy. The few local peace officers still willing to talk to me had told me of lead after lead that had turned out to be bullshit, in the same category as sightings of Elvis, UFOs, Abe Lincoln's ghost, and the like. People all over Ohio and adjacent states were convinced they'd seen Donny Blackmon.

I didn't want any part of this case.

"Ms. Blackmon, I'll be honest with you. I have read your husband's blog. I do not like your husband very much, based just on that. But there's more, of course. They found your husband's gun near the body, on your property. Your husband hates cops. If I did find your husband, I would drag his ass back to Mifflin County to stand trial."

"I don't want you to do that." There was a hint of pride in her face as she said it, like she doubted I'd be able to do it. And maybe she was right. I'd seen the photos and the videos on his blog. Her husband was a big guy, a burly fellow with a thick beard who could have

been cast as a lumberjack. I'm a big guy, too, and I work out, but . . .
maybe she was right. When you go into a fight, there are no
guarantees.

Donny also was a gun collector, and so were many of his friends.
That was another reason to stay the hell out of it.

I blew out the breath I'd been holding. "I'd bring him in anyway,"
I said, "whether you wanted me to or not. He's a suspect in the murder of a police officer."

"I just want you to find him, not bring him back."

I shrugged. "The cops are going to find him, eventually. You don't
need me."

Her jaw quivered. "Yes, I do. I want you to find him before they
do. I want you to give him a message."

I did not feel like being anyone's errand boy. "You have no way of
contacting him? Excuse me, but I find that a little difficult to
believe."

She shook her head. "He didn't take no phone, no credit cards,
no nothing," she said. "He didn't tell me where he was going. That
was so the cops could not torture it out of me."

"No cop is going to—"

"Hell no, they're not going to!"

I sighed. "If there is nothing to go on, I'm not sure where to start.
What is this message you want me to deliver?"

Her throat contracted, and she had trouble getting out the words.
"Tell him it's Cassie."

Cassie was the nine-year-old daughter Donny Blackmon had run
out on. "What about Cassie?"

"She's dying."

I stared at the woman and had absolutely no idea what to say or
how to say it.

"It's cancer," she said after a long pause. "Ain't nothing they can do, probably, except some experimental stuff. We can't afford it. Church is going to help us with that part of it, the money and the prayers, but..."

"I am sorry to hear this," I said. I remembered the photos of the little girl with all the news stories about the murder, the ones they always write to tell people more about the suspect so everybody can satisfy their morbid curiosity and ask themselves how such things can happen. I'm not judging anyone here. I read those stories, too.

Cassie was a little version of her mother, without all the cares showing on her face. The kind of little girl you expected to see hugging Cinderella at Disney World.

Mrs. Blackmon's pause showed no sign of letting up, so I nudged her. "But what?"

"Donny don't know," Amy Blackmon said. The tears started then. "We just found out, after he run off. Donny don't know. I want you to find him, and tell him. Tell him Cassie is sick. Then he'll find a way to see his girl."

I was dumbfounded. "I don't know..."

"Please," she said. "Donny's got to know."

I shook my head slowly back and forth. "I'm sure if you tell the news people, Donny will see it..."

"Hell no!" The eyes widened, and she inhaled sharply, ready for a fight. "The press? Are you seriously saying that?"

"I just thought—"

"After what they done to Donny? He's tried and convicted! And they already put Cassie's picture in there. I never told them they could. It was a school picture. I am not going to let them do anything to her, not going to see all the shit people will say online, how we're just faking the cancer for sympathy, for... for money! Hell no!"

I nodded. "I understand. Sure. OK."

She took a few seconds to calm down, then sighed. "Donny wouldn't believe anything the damned press said anyway, no way no how. He'd just think it is a trap. He ain't stupid. But he's got to find out about Cassie. You find him. You tell him. I'll give you a letter, you give it to him. He'll believe you if you show him that."

"Well," I said, unable to come up with anything better in the moment. I was saved from deciding what to say by an interruption.

"Mommy?"

It was a girl's voice. Cassie was standing in the kitchen doorway.

Moms are the most amazing people on Earth. Amy Blackmon inhaled sharply and got herself under control, in less time than it took a heart to beat. She wiped away tears with her hands, quickly and efficiently, before she turned to face her daughter. I could tell she'd done this many times before. I don't think Cassie noticed mom had been crying at all. "Yes, baby?"

"Did you call me?"

"I just said your name for Mr. Runyon here. He's a private investigator. I'm hoping to convince him to go find Daddy."

Cassie was small for a nine-year-old. If I'd been guessing her age at a carnival, I'd have said seven, maybe even six. She looked at me. "Please? Can you go find Daddy?"

Fuck.

CHAPTER TWO

You might as well know this. Kids are my kryptonite.

I started Whiskey River Investigations, the one-man agency I run in Ohio farm country, after leaving my job as a detective with the Mifflin County Sheriff's Office. I left that job because too many missing kid cases fell through the cracks amid all the other things a public servant has to deal with. Well, there were other reasons, too, but that's the important one. I had a couple of missing kid cases go horribly wrong. It messed me up, honestly, and I am still dealing with that. Part of coping meant striking out on my own as a private investigator who specializes in finding missing kids.

Donny Blackmon was no kid, of course, but Cassie was. As much as I wanted to run like hell from this case, I am just not capable of ignoring a plea from a nine-year-old girl with cancer.

Like I said, kids are my kryptonite.

There was another thing to consider, too. My bank account was getting mighty damned slim. I was paying bills, but not making much profit. Private investigators don't drum up a ton of business in rural Ohio, but I was too stubborn to move to one of the big cities.

Amy hustled her daughter into a back bedroom, and I could hear them whispering, but I could not make out the words. Being alone for a moment gave me a chance to notice how the air-conditioning was losing the battle against this day's Ohio heat. I hoped tomorrow would be cooler, and, this being Ohio, there was a good chance. Us Buckeyes say it all the time. Don't like the weather? Just wait a minute. It'll change.

Being alone gave me a chance to muster my reasons for not taking on this case. Donny Blackmon might have killed a cop. I used to be a cop. A lot of my friends are cops. And even if Blackmon wasn't guilty, he'd sure written a lot of nasty things about cops on his damned blog. He accused cops of murder, rape, shooting and sniffing confiscated drugs, shaking down small business owners for money if they ever expected a police officer to show up when needed. You name it—if it was bad, Donny Blackmon accused cops of doing it.

I was predisposed to not like Donny Blackmon one goddamned bit, and now that his daughter was no longer staring at me with big blue eyes, I was able to think clearly.

I had made up my mind by the time Amy Blackmon returned to the kitchen. "I didn't really mean for Cassie to overhear any of that," she said.

"I understand. She seems like a brave girl."

Amy's whole face shuddered, but just for a microsecond. "Braver than her mom."

I kept my mouth shut for a moment. Then I told her the truth. "Ma'am, I do not want to take this case. Your husband has not been kind to law enforcement. To be honest, after reading some of the stuff he's written, I've daydreamed about breaking his nose."

She nodded. "I get that. Donny can be a handful, and he ain't afraid to speak his mind. But he is not dangerous, I swear it. He believes in free speech and reason, not force. Not murder."

I used my thumb to point over my shoulder, toward the living room we'd walked through when I arrived. "There is a lot of firepower in there that would suggest otherwise." Her husband had cases with glass doors mounted on every wall, and the room looked like the display floor of a gun shop. Rifles, handguns, shotguns, you name it. Donny Blackmon had three or four of each. His wife had told me he had a lot more in the basement.

"Oh, Donny likes his guns, and anyone who broke into this house or threatened this family in any way was gonna find out he knows how to use them," she said, with more than a hint of pride. "His wife knows how to use them, too, and we're teaching Cassie. But Donny don't go around threatening people. He feels safe living around here, calls it God's country. Figures all the guns he writes about on his blog and all the pictures would keep most fools from trying anything here."

Indeed, the *Blackmon Report* regularly featured a "Gun of the Week," usually with video of Donny waxing poetic about how much he loved his Ruger this or his Sig Sauer that. Other people came on as guests to shoot with Donny or show off their own guns. Donny was a gun nut.

I pushed my unfinished coffee aside. "OK. Duly noted. Donny isn't dangerous." I'm fairly certain my expression said otherwise, but I'm seldom good at controlling that. "I notice he hasn't blogged since he vanished."

"Of course not," she replied. "He ain't a fool. He won't touch the blog, nor the whole internet, because he don't want to leave a trace. Hell, he won't even use a library computer to send me an email. He knows shit like that can be traced, and he knows every cop in the country would shoot him on sight."

I bristled at that. "Or, you know, take him into custody to face a fair trial."

She actually sneered. "Sure."

We stared at one another for a little while, until she broke the silence.

"Don't do it for Donny," she said, "or for me. Do it for my girl."

Fuck.

"I am not promising to take this case," I said. "I need to think about this."

She nodded. "I can understand that, I guess."

I went on. "I am no fan of your husband."

She shook her head. "Few people are."

"I want you to show me where the officer was found dead."

"Sure. Follow me."

She went into the back hall and I followed. We passed Cassie's room. The girl was tickling a huge stuffed rabbit. Beyond that, at the next door, I saw something that made me pause.

I pointed. "Are those Martin guitars?"

Amy stopped and turned back to face me. "Yeah, Donny picks them. He's pretty good. You play?"

"I strum a little," I said. "Mind if I look around in here?"

"Go ahead."

I stepped into the room and got a little jealous and a little sad. Four Martin guitars were mounted on the wall, each a pristine work of art. The music they would make in capable hands would be art, too. Carter Stanley, Tony Rice, Norman Blake, Bryan Sutton—all of those stellar pickers had played Martin D-28s.

One of Donny Blackmon's had words scrawled in Sharpie ink across the face: "I played this. It sounds beautiful. Tony Rice, July 20, 1983."

"Wow," I said. "Tony was a hell of a picker. Bluegrass legend."

I tried not to think of the Martin I'd once owned.

Amy Blackmon stepped up next to me. "Donny won't play that one." She pointed at the Tony Rice guitar. "He won it in a festival auction. Probably misses that guitar more than he misses me. Loves his guitars more than his guns, even."

The other walls were decorated with album covers. Doc Watson, Bill Monroe, Del McCoury, the Osborne Brothers, Sam Bush, John Hartford, and other legends of bluegrass and folk music. The only furnishings in the room were a comfortable chair, a shelf full of vinyl records, a table with a record player on it, and a couple of speakers. The chair and the curtains smelled like cigarette smoke, and the table had plenty of rings left by plenty of shot glasses.

"I guess I'll be selling these," she said, quietly. "The guns, too. We need the money." She looked at me. "Would you take a guitar in payment?"

I gulped. The Martin I was trying not to think about had been a gift from my father. I'd busted it during a moment of depressive rage a while back. That memory surfaced like a Kraken when I saw Donny Blackmon's guitars, and now that I was being offered one, everything in me tightened up. I took a deep breath.

"I think you should auction the guitars," I said. "You should get good prices on them."

I didn't mention selling the guns. She could get good money for those, of course, and probably could sell them faster than the instruments. Part of me wondered who might buy the weapons, though, and what they might do with them. I'm all for self-defense, and I've eaten my share of venison and rabbit taken by local hunters. I have met too many people, though, who seem to almost hope somebody messes with them so they can whip out that gun and pretend they are Clint Eastwood. And don't get me started on the mass shootings. To put it bluntly, this country is fucking crazy when it comes to guns.

I wasn't going to solve that problem, though, so I concentrated on the other problem I probably couldn't solve—finding Donny Blackmon.

"Does Donny play music with anyone?"

She nodded. "He jams with Tug Burrell, a few others. They all try to get him to do gigs, but Donny usually don't want to, unless it's an emergency and they need somebody right now. He just wants to play with buddies, maybe try to play some stuff that's hard to play. He'd rather do that and screw it up than play the same fifteen songs perfectly for a crowd every night, he says."

"Well, it must be nice to be able to do that. Did he take a guitar with him?"

"None missing from the house."

"OK."

She went back into the hall and headed toward a rear door. I followed her out.

CHAPTER THREE

IT WAS A late Sunday morning in June, and we were walking almost a mile down a dirt lane between a field with corn leaves just peeping up through the ground and a grove of oaks and black locust bordered by ditch lilies that showed signs of imminent blooming. It was way too hot to be hiking since the woods were on the wrong side of the road to give us any shade, but that's what we were doing.

Beyond the lilies, a thick bed of jewelweed covered the ground beneath the towering trees. Dots of orange fire were easy to see among all the green and shadow. A gray squirrel clung to an oak, staring at us. Such scenes are why I work in Mifflin County instead of moving my PI agency to the more lucrative cities of Columbus or Cleveland, as Linda has often urged me to do. She had backed off on saying such things lately, now that we were living together and had gone totally exclusive, as they say, but she still rolls her eyes now and then at my notion that I can make a go of this business in the middle of Ohio farm country. *How often do the Amish hire private investigators*, she'd asked me once. *Not as often as I'd like*, I'd replied. But I work cheap, and I can travel. I scrape by. And everything's online now anyway. I have a website and a phone. Clients find me. Not many of them, so far, but a man can dream.

"Our property on the left," Amy said, pointing, "and Del Palmer's on the right, with all the trees."

"And the barn where you found the officer is ahead? On this road?"

She nodded.

I thought about that. There did not seem to be any easy way to get to the barn without trampling corn or dealing with underbrush, unless you took this road.

I recalled details from the news reports. Officer Gullick had been wearing a T-shirt, sweatpants, and sneakers. His wife had said it was his habit to run early every morning. His own service weapon had not been found at the scene, nor had there been any indications of any bullets from any gun other than the one that had killed him. And Gullick's car had been in his own driveway at the time.

I resumed asking questions. "So, Donny gave you no indication at all that he was going on the run?"

"No, sir, he did not. He just up and went."

"Does that surprise you? I mean, wouldn't he want to say goodbye, explain things?"

She turned her head and sneered at me. "No, it does not surprise me even a little bit, since a dead cop was found on our farm with one of Donny's guns laying there. Donny ain't a fool. He don't trust cops, he don't trust courts, and he knows how the law feels about him for telling the truth. He went out to the barn to work on his tractor, and I'm guessing he found a dead cop by the barn and ran like hell. They are trying to frame him, Mr. Runyon. They set him up. He knew I'd figure it out, and he knew I'd understand. I ain't no fool, either."

"They found his gun at the scene," I said. The gun was a Sig Sauer P226 MK25, beloved by Navy SEALs and featured not once, but twice, on the *Blackmon Report*. He had purchased it used, and it had a couple of scratches on the barrel. Those scratches were clearly visible on his blog video, and, according to news reports, they had led Mifflin County Sheriff's Office detectives to ask Amy Blackmon if the murder weapon was Donny's gun. Detective Scott Baxter, a friend of mine, had told me over beers that Amy Blackmon had not hesitated to identify the weapon. "Steady as hell," he'd said, "like a hawk staring down at a bull." I had no idea why Bax put it that way since hawks and bulls pay no attention to one another, but he has a way of bungling metaphors that everyone just sort of accepts, because conversations get sidetracked if you ask him to explain. It's better to just roll with it.

"She didn't even blink," Bax had told me. "'That's Donny's gun,' she said, 'but he didn't kill him.' I almost believed her. Almost."

She did have an honest air about her, I had to admit. But I remember a guy in an Ambletown bar once who looked trustworthy, too, just before he punched me in the face. I won that fight, by the way, and I was an off-duty sheriff's detective at the time so I had to work pretty hard to make sure none of it went on public record. So don't ask me any more about it. Anyway, an honest face proves nothing.

"Yes, they did find his gun," she said, in answer to my question. "His gun, for sure. Some son of a bitch planted it there."

"How could someone else have gotten their hands on the gun?"

She shook her head. "No idea. But someone did."

I shooed away a pesky fly. "There were no break-ins, no burglaries reported at your house?"

"Nope," she said. "My best guess is he sold it to someone. He was always doing gun shows, and now and then he'd do a sale on the side, someone would ask about buying a gun, and he'd meet them somewhere. Maybe he sold that one. I don't keep track. I don't love them the way Donny does. But I told the deputies that. I told them he probably sold it. They didn't give a shit what I said. They'd already made up their minds."

"I saw his blogs about that gun," I said. "He loved that gun. Would he really sell it?"

"Donny would sell his left nut to support his family, and we always need money," she said. "Donny did factory work and made good money, until that went away. Then he did small engine repair, from home. That brought in some money but no insurance. And the farming. Donny does some, just feed corn, and we lease out some of the land to local farmers. Family farming is not a moneymaker these days, at least not reliable. It's all big-ass egg farms, big-ass corporate chicken farms, you name it, and you have to fight the weather and the bugs. Hell yes, he'd sell the gun, if the price was right. He loves us more than his guns. I'm probably going to sell them all."

"Duly noted," I said.

"Probably selling some of the land, too," she said, weeping softly. "Been in his family forever."

We walked on, past some peonies that had shriveled like vampires under the hot June sun. I glanced at the sky and realized there was no chance at all of a refreshing rain. I wiped away sweat from my forehead. Despite the heat, I still love Ohio.

A big barn, sorely in need of paint and some replacement planks, loomed ahead of us. My guide pointed. "That's where I found him, by the barn."

You see barns all over this part of Ohio. The bright red ones with bright white trim usually end up on calendar photos. The Amish barns go on calendars and tourism websites. The old dilapidated ones, slowly falling apart because everything eventually does, tend to inspire fine-art photography.

The Blackmon barn probably was destined to appear on a true crime blog.

There was still tape marking off the crime scene. I stopped Amy before we got too close. I didn't want to step on anything the forensic team might have missed, even though I doubted they'd missed anything. Those people are pretty damned thorough.

Amy Blackmon pointed. "The dead man was right there, against the barn. You can see the stain."

Indeed, I could see the bloodstain. It was hard to miss, a dark smear across gray wood, with streamers running down along the grain. Officer Brandon Gullick had taken two shots to the head. Head wounds bleed a lot.

"I was taking Donny some lemonade," she said, softly. "He gets thirsty when he's working. Anyway, that's when I found the body."

She didn't shudder when she recollected that moment. She had other, more terrifying things on her mind.

"And you called the sheriff?"

"I did."

"But you and Donny don't trust the sheriff."

"No," she answered. Then she sighed. "But I ain't never found a dead body before. You find a body, you call the cops, right? Donny was not around, and I didn't know anything else to do. And I sure as hell wasn't gonna clean up that mess and bury the body myself, was I?"

"I guess not."

I looked over the landscape. It was perfectly pastoral in the late morning light. The barn, and the rolling land surrounding it, would have made a really nice postcard if you didn't know it was a murder scene.

"And the cops found the gun, and you identified it," I said.

"Yes," she replied. "I ain't a liar. Like I told you, I'm guessing Donny sold it."

"Did he keep records of sales?"

She spat on the ground. "Not really. I mean, he had a notebook for that, but he wasn't real good at keeping track. I looked, believe me. No sign he sold it. But he must have."

I started rolling a bunch of coincidences around in my mind. Donny sells gun, said gun ends up being found at a murder scene on Donny's farm, next to a dead cop, and, by the way, Donny hates cops.

"Donny's print was on the gun," I said.

"A partial print," she said, quickly. "And he owned the gun, so, you know, duh. No big surprise his print was on it."

"Big surprise it was found next to a dead cop, though," I said. She ignored that.

She pointed. "Stray bullet hit there," she said, and I noticed a small hole in the barn wall.

"If I recall correctly," I said, knowing damn well I recalled correctly but I wanted to see how she reacted, "there were signs that the officer had been in a fight, before he got shot." Officer Gullick's hair and blood were found on a two-by-four at the scene.

"Yeah," she said. "Cops said someone had clubbed him with a piece of wood or something, back here." She reached behind her head and patted her uncombed hair. "Donny's more of a break-his-fucking-nose guy, to be honest. I don't see him doing the sneaky thing, you know? From behind? Ain't his way."

"OK." She'd said all that in a matter-of-fact way, very confidently, like she was quoting the Gospel of Mark and absolutely convinced it was true. I was not at all convinced that Donny Blackmon had not killed Officer Brandon Gullick, but I was quite certain Amy Blackmon believed her husband was innocent.

I surveyed the scene, and my imagination added Officer Gullick and his killer. I tried to envision how it might have happened, or why Officer Gullick would have come out here. Or why, if he was guilty, Donny Blackmon would leave behind his precious gun.

The road we'd walked on kept going on past the barn.

"Does that connect to Dream Road?"

"Yes," she answered. "It wraps around Oscar Boone's place, then connects up on Dream. About two miles, I guess."

So someone could have approached the barn from that direction without going near the Blackmon house. That meant someone could have knocked Brandon Gullick silly, driven the unconscious man along back roads, and brought him here to put two bullets in his head. But if that's how it had happened, the bloodstains were an anomaly. Gullick was standing up when he was shot. The killer would have had to wait for Gullick to wake up, so he could stand up.

None of that made sense. Why beat a man and then wait for him to wake up and gain his feet if you were planning to just kill him? And if you didn't drag the victim here, well, how did he get here? Some sort of rendezvous? Some sort of trap? What would lure Gullick out here?

Maybe Gullick came out here voluntarily, with his killer. Or maybe Gullick came here for reasons of his own, and Donny killed him.

I let it spin around in my head, but the Magic 8-Ball in my skull did not pop up a clear answer. Would Gullick have gone to a cop hater's farm unarmed, in his running clothes? Would Donny have dragged the guy out to his own property to kill him, when Mifflin County has acres of woodland and several deep creeks highly suitable for dumping bodies?

I wanted to run, go open a beer, and forget I'd ever answered Amy Blackmon's phone call.

But then an image of Cassie flashed in my mind. "Did you hear the shots?"

She shook her head. "No, I don't remember any, and even if I did, I wouldn't hardly have noticed. Donny shoots, other people shoot, there's hunters. You just don't notice that kind of thing all that much around here, you know?"

"Yeah." I knew what she meant. I'd lived in a rented pond-side trailer in the woods before moving in with Linda at her family's farmhouse, and both spots were far enough from town to make gunshots a common sound. Not that you need to be very far from town to hear guns in Mifflin County, anyway. People around here shoot at critters and targets all the time.

"News reports said the coroner put the time of death at about six a.m., give or take some. Were you home then?"

"Yeah. Don't remember hearing nothing, though."

"Did you see anything? Cars, trucks, anybody walking?"

"No. I told all this to the sheriffs."

Indeed, Bax had told me she'd been very cooperative. I sighed. "I am still not sure I want to take this case," I said.

"I ain't sure who else I can ask," she replied. "Ain't no one can help Cassie, I guess."

I stared at her and wished she had not mentioned her daughter. I envisioned Cassie, all wide-eyed innocence staring at the rapidly approaching end of time, standing in the hallway and asking me to please go find her daddy.

I sighed again. "I gotta think about this."

"I understand," Amy Blackmon said. "If it is money, well, the church is helping us out and I'll find a way to pay you."

I shook my head. "It's not the money."

We walked back to the house in silence, save for the occasional comment about the heat or the swarming midges or the zooming cardinals. I promised to give her an answer soon, then I got into my truck and fired up a Sam Bush CD. I had a lot of thinking to do.

The first question I asked was how a loving God could create a universe where children get cancer. I had no idea. I suppose I could have asked a preacher, but the answer probably would just be that it was somehow humanity's fault. Original sin, or something like it. I don't know. Seemed to me God could have figured out something better, but I'm no expert.

The next question, of course, was how could I explain to Linda that I was maybe going to go look for a gun nut who had possibly murdered a cop?

She was not going to like that. Not at all.

CHAPTER FOUR

UNDER NORMAL CIRCUMSTANCES when faced with a tough decision, I'd have stopped at Tuck's Bar and Grill in the tiny one-traffic-light town of Jodyville and endured the popular "country music" from the jukebox so I could consult with my friend, the owner, and lubricate my gray cells with a beer or two. But this was Sunday, and the bar was closed, so I trudged up the white stairs along the exterior wall of the bar that led to the apartments above.

That's where I'd find James Tiberius Tucker, probably listening to heavy metal that was just as bad as the bar music in my mind, but a necessary cleanser for Tuck after a week of playing music he hates but his customers love. Tuck is a much better businessman than I am. He figures out what people want and gives it to them for a fair price. I tend to chase half of my potential clients away because some of them are assholes. It's not a great business model, I admit.

I could just make out a heavy drone of bass and drums and somebody growling. No hint of a tune, and it didn't seem to me the performer cared whether anyone could understand the lyrics.

I was going to need a heavy dose of Waylon Jennings after this.

I looked around at what passes for downtown in Jodyville. Aside from Tuck's bar, there were five antique stores—some tend to come and go, others have been here for decades—and the corner market that features awesome fry pies. I sighed when I saw the empty porch swing at Nancy's house. She had been a nice old lady, beating me at checkers and always trying to get me to attend her church. She had passed early in the year.

After my reverie, I knocked, and the infernal music within died. Tuck opened the door, his black face shining with sweat. He was in shorts and a T-shirt, and obviously had been working out. It had been a while since I'd seen him, and I was surprised to see all the beads in his hair gone. It was still long, though. He had it pulled back in a ponytail. "Hey, Ed, c'mon in."

"Your neighbor on the other side of the wall must be away. You had it turned up mighty loud."

He picked up a towel from the back of a chair. "Yeah, no need for headphones today," he replied. "She's off somewhere. I've been running in place. Nice to have some music that gets the heart pumping!"

"I can lend you some Béla Fleck banjo music," I told him. "That'll get you going. And you can always go run around the pond like I do. Way more scenic."

"I don't want to trip over tree roots or beavers or teen lovers or anything like that," he said. "Anyway, I'm trying to work off the beers. Owning a bar is a constant temptation for a beer nerd like me. Want one?"

"Sure," I said. I looked around while he went to the kitchen, examining his stacks of books to see if there was anything I wanted to borrow. He had one by Robin Yocum I had not read yet, so I made a mental note.

Tuck came back with two bottles of 90 Minute IPA from Dogfish Head Craft Brewery. I took one gladly, thankful that it was a beer I already knew. Tuck is a beer evangelist and is always trying to get me to try something different. I prefer the tried and true, but I did have to give him credit for introducing me to the Dogfish. It is a fine hoppy elixir, and Tuck manages not to gloat when he sees me drink one. He's a good guy, although I seldom admit that in front of him.

"I hate to dispense with proper glasses," he said, "but I just started the dishwasher."

"No problem." I told him about my talk with Amy Blackmon.

"Damn," he said. "That's rough, I know. Linda is gonna worry."

"Yeah."

"But you're gonna do it, right? Find that girl's dad?"

"I don't know."

"Don't you?" He took a deep swig from his bottle.

"You think I've already made up my mind."

He nodded. "Yes, I do. One, it's a kid. You always melt with kids. Big Mister Tough Guy, gimme my real Johnny Cash music and don't mess with me when it comes to everyone else. But a sick kid, wants her dad? You'll say yes. Number two, if you were going to say no, you would not be here now. You'd be at home with Linda, probably grilling something delicious and listening to something way too twangy for human consumption and not wearing that worried face."

"You're probably right," I admitted.

"Of course I'm right. So how do you think she'll take it?"

I shook my head. "She talked about that Blackmon case nonstop when it happened, about how scary Donny Blackmon was and how glad she was I had quit the sheriff's department, like Blackmon was a serial killer targeting cops," I said. "She said if I was still on the SO, and still on the SWAT team, I'd end up going up against Donny and all his gun-loving friends. She was real glad I was not still a sheriff's detective."

"Yeah," Tuck said. "She's said some of the same to me. I'm not sure she's all wrong."

"Maybe, maybe not." I finished my beer. "But that little girl wants to see her daddy before . . . well, before."

"Yeah."

"So I guess I have to be a man and go tell Linda what I'm going to do, and why."

Tuck nodded. "Guess so. I think you are doing the right thing, by the way."

"You do?"

"Yes, I do. Innocent until proven guilty, of course, and while it doesn't look good for Donny Blackmon being innocent, he hasn't stood trial. Innocent or guilty, that little girl loves her dad. You're doing it for her, not for him."

"Of course. But to be honest, it isn't an ironclad case. There's a lot of incongruous stuff that just doesn't mesh if Donny really killed him."

"Yeah?"

I filled him in on some of my concerns.

"So, you'll figure it out. You're a good detective, Ed."

"Thanks."

"All the same, it could be trouble."

I shook my head. "I don't know, Tuck. This guy didn't even tell his wife where he went, if she is telling the truth, and I think she is or else why would she hire me? I doubt he told his gun-loving patriot buddies where he went. I'm not walking into a machine gun nest or anything. I'm probably not going to find him at all. I have no idea where to start looking."

"His wife is here, Ed, where he thinks the cops can torture her and steal her secrets. Cops can't do that to his buddies unless they know who his buddies are. His blog had a long reach, lots of views. He would need help, I would think, unless he's gone totally Grizzly

Adams. He probably has friends helping him, and they could be friends far from here. Loyal blog readers, helping out their hero."

"Well," I said, "you may be right. Thanks for the shoulder and the beer."

"Anytime. Good luck with Linda."

"Thanks. I'm going to need it. Unless I can talk myself out of doing this. And I'm going to try."

"You'll take the job," Tuck said.

"When I'm done, can I borrow the Yocum?" I pointed at the book.

"Sure, man. You'll dig it."

I closed the door behind me.

CHAPTER FIVE

I DROVE BETWEEN cornfields on one side and thick woods on the other, thinking about the scene where Brandon Gullick had been shot dead. The big sticking point, for me, was figuring out why the officer was on the Blackmon farm in the first place.

The farm was in the jurisdiction of the Mifflin County Sheriff's Office, not the Ambletown Police Department that employed Gullick, so it was unlikely that Gullick was investigating a crime. Criminal activity sometimes ignores boundaries, of course, and agencies cooperate, but it would be unusual for a city cop to investigate something in the county's purview without at least checking in with the SO, and ordinarily there would have been a deputy there, too. Detective Scott Baxter had told me no one at the SO knew of anything Gullick might have been investigating at the Blackmon place, and said he'd asked Ambletown PD about it himself. No one there knew anything, either.

So why had Gullick been there? Had he gone out to confront Donny about something written on his blog, some smear against law enforcement? Unlikely. Nobody thought of Brandon Gullick as a hothead. By all accounts, he was a good cop and kept his cool. That was a trick I had not always been good at when I was a cop, but I feel like I'm better at it now that I work for myself and can control the workload.

The Blackmon farm was at least a dozen miles from the Gullick home, but the slain man was known to run in the country and he'd run a marathon or two. He'd been a cross-country star in high school.

I was going to have to look at reports Bax and the other detectives had written and talk to Bax again. I was not eager to do that, because they might not take kindly to me poking into this particular case. The cops I'd talked to were hard set on handling this themselves. Brandon Gullick had been one of their own.

I rounded a bend, slowed down for a buzzard eating a rabbit in the middle of the road, and popped a Willie Nelson CD into the player. I hit SHUFFLE, and "Good-Hearted Woman" filled the air. I cranked it up. I was on my way to see my woman, who could star as a leading lady in a James Bond movie if she wanted to, but she hates those flicks and says they portray women as sex objects. She's right, of course, but I watch them anyway. I like the explosions, and I like looking at Daniela Bianchi parading around in lingerie in *From Russia with Love*. Sue me.

Anyway, Linda has long legs and red hair and flashing green eyes, and she helped me get through some pretty tough times. I'm lucky to have her, and I wouldn't trade her for anyone. Not even Daniela Bianchi.

But Linda was going to read me the riot act when I told her about this case. Hell, she might even get mad enough to leave me for a Bond girl. Linda's sexual attractions are more wide-ranging than mine. Tuck says that means I have to be even more attentive and loving to my girl than other guys, because Linda has more options than some. I think Tuck's full of shit, but I try to be better than I probably am because I'd like to keep her.

Life is complex, ain't it?

Willie was singing about how the good-hearted woman loves her man even though she doesn't quite understand all the things he does. Man, I hope that's the case.

CHAPTER SIX

"FUCK YES, YOU should do it," Linda said.

She was kneeling by a garden bed, pulling weeds so her bee balm and daylilies could thrive. A pitcher of lemonade stood on a paver beside her. I picked it up and took a drink. It was laced with vodka.

"Don't drink straight from the pitcher, barbarian," she said. "Go get a glass."

"One sip is enough for me, thanks," I said. I'm not a vodka guy.

"Anyway, how could you not try to find him? His daughter is dying, Ed. He needs to know."

"I have no goddamned idea how I'm going to find him."

She looked up at me and smiled. "You will figure it out."

"It is entirely possible your faith in me is misplaced." I knelt nearby and started pulling weeds, too.

"No, it's not. Don't pull that one. It's not a weed."

I pulled back my hand from the green sprout I had nearly yanked from the soil. "What is it?"

"No idea," she said. "But I don't think it's a weed. It's a volunteer. I didn't plant it, it's just something wild. Let it grow, and we can pull it later if it isn't beautiful."

"OK. So you really think I should take this case?"

She wiped her brow with the back of her arm. "I am not Donny Blackmon's biggest fan, I'll admit. The way he writes about guns, I think he wants to fuck them. He's a total ammosexual."

"OK."

"But I met Cassie. When my students visited the elementaries and the middle school to do scenes from *Romeo and Juliet*. She is such a sweet kid, and she loved the show. I mean loved. She did the whole 'wherefore art thou, Romeo' bit with her hands clutched in front of her chest and her eyes aimed heavenward and her voice all singsong, and she told me she'd never heard it or read it before, but she memorized it that quick. She's an amazing kid. Hell yes, Ed, go find her dad for her."

"He doesn't want to be found. He might shoot me."

She blew a wayward strand of red hair out of her face. "I don't want you to get close to him, you idiot. Just figure out where he is and send him a postcard, or call him. Keep your distance. Stay out of gun range. But let him know his little girl needs to see him."

"Well," I replied, "this is not at all the reaction I expected."

She smiled. "Do the job, don't get shot, OK?"

"Don't get shot *again*, you mean." I still have a nasty scar down my back from a bullet I'd taken while hunting for Jimmy Zachman. It still hurts, from time to time.

"Don't get shot ever again," she said, putting a ton of emphasis on the word "ever." She leaned over and kissed me. "Be smart, be safe, but find her dad."

"OK," I said. "I might do it." I pointed. "Is that one a weed?"

Linda nodded. "Get it out of there."

We pulled weeds and chatted for a half hour or so. "Since I'm already a sweaty mess," I said, "I'm going to go for a run. Need to clear my head."

She nodded. "Yep, go do some thinking. Then call Ms. Blackmon and tell her you are taking the job. I'm going to go shower once I'm done here. Don't forget Shelly and Lana are coming by. They say it'll be late in the day, so you've got time."

"Thanks for the reminder."

Shelly is Michelle Beckworth, a Columbus Police Department detective who was around when I went a little nuts chasing after a guy who'd killed a teen girl a while back. Lana is an actress-model-dancer, and Shelly's girlfriend.

I gave Linda a kiss, stepped inside, pulled my duffel from the closet, and headed to my truck. "I won't be too long."

I was headed to the large pond by the trailer I used to rent in the middle of not much of anything, before moving in with Linda. I like running laps around it. Ducking branches and leaping over roots is good reflex training, and there is no traffic unless you count the occasional whitetail or squirrel. It was a good routine, and I do my best thinking there.

As I rounded past some cattails on the far side of the pond, I noted a newcomer. A large blue heron stood in shallows up to his knees, his fierce eyes glaring at the water. I stopped as quietly as I could, hoping not to startle him, then settled down on a fallen tree to watch.

I wondered if his dinosaur ancestors had hunted the same way, standing still as the prey swam about their legs. I was hoping to see his sharp beak spear into the pond and come up with a bluegill, but I had no such luck. Ten minutes or so after I'd spotted him, the heron swooped the huge wings and lifted into the sky.

No luck for the big bird in this spot.

I wondered if it was an omen. Maybe the universe was telling me I'd have no better luck seeking Donny Blackmon. Maybe there was no point in looking for the cop-hating blogger and potentially meeting his gun-loving friends.

I jogged the rest of the way around the pond—it's really a lake, but the folks who own it call it a pond—and stopped short at my second surprise of the day.

There was an SUV parked next to my truck and a tall man leaning against it. He wore dark slacks, a blue dress shirt with the sleeves rolled up, and a gaudy red tie that was loose around the neck. His shoes were not the sort one wears when wandering about in the country, and his sunglasses were a bit too large. They kept slipping down his beak of a nose, and he had to keep adjusting them.

He had a holstered pistol, clipped to his belt.

"Ed Runyon?"

I nodded. "Yes. I don't think I know you."

"Detective Jim Lannigan, Ambletown PD." He pulled a leather case from his rear pocket and flashed the badge.

"You must be kind of new," I said.

"Yeah." He nodded. "Started seven months ago, moved here from Columbus."

"Kind of a big change," I said. "Much smaller town."

Lannigan shrugged. "Crime is crime, I suppose. My wife took a position teaching at the college." He meant Ambletown College, a small independent college that mostly turned out teachers and business majors. "I followed along."

"Welcome to Mifflin County. What can I do for you? And how did you find me? This place is a little out of the way."

He removed the sunglasses. His eyes were a sharp green, rather steady and piercing. The kind of eyes Robin Hood might have fixed on his target. "I was told you lived out on a farm. I checked there, and your lady told me where to look." He continued to stare at me, and the closer I got, the less friendly he looked.

"Well, that was easy enough. So why are you looking for me?"

He stood up straight. "You are going to tell me where the fuck Donny Blackmon is."

CHAPTER SEVEN

My normal, knee-jerk reaction when someone tells me what the fuck I'm going to do is to tell them exactly why the fuck they are wrong, but I reminded myself that this man was investigating the murder of a cop. That kind of thing can make cops edgy even when they don't intend to be, so I gave him a polite answer.

"I have no idea where Donny Blackmon is, Detective."

He stepped toward me, slipping the sunglasses into his shirt pocket. Between the sharp green eyes and the beak nose, he reminded me a bit of the heron. The heron's eyes were yellow, but whatever. There was a resemblance. "Is that a fact, Mr. Runyon?"

I stopped walking, and stood up straight. "It is, indeed."

We stood facing each other, about ten feet apart. Nothing in his stance told me I should be ready for a fight, but his attitude was combative nonetheless. "I know you talked to Blackmon's wife this morning."

This did not surprise me. When a police officer is killed, the chief suspect's home remains under surveillance, even if it takes months. The police probably knew exactly when I showed up at the Blackmon farm and exactly how long I stayed. If I'd been setting up surveillance, I'd have camped on one of three hills overlooking the Blackmon farm. With a telescope or a good set of binoculars, you'd be able to see anyone coming and going. The roads leading there were pretty easy to spy on, too. Lots of copses and barns for spies to hide in along the way.

Hell, I'd have had drones with cameras over the place at all hours, if possible.

I saw no reason to play hard to get. "Yes, sir, I did talk to her."

"Were you delivering a message from Donny?"

"I've never met Donny," I replied. "I wasn't delivering anything."

"You a family friend, then? Or fooling around with his wife while he's off hiding?"

I grinned and shook my head. "I've been patient up to now, Detective Lannigan. Folks who know me best would say you should not count on that continuing."

He spat on the grass. "Not up there with your boyish charm, consoling the lonely woman, huh?"

I've been told many times I look a bit like the late actor Heath Ledger. I don't quite see it myself. But in any case, I don't spend time moving in on another man's wife when he's away. "Lannigan, you are starting to piss me off. I hope this behavior of yours is just your idea of an off-putting interrogation technique and that you're really not this big of an asshole. But, just so you know, despite my hard run I'm pretty sure I have enough fuel in the tank to kick your ass if you keep this up."

He grinned, still looking a bit like a heron poised over a bluegill, and thought about it. "So, what then? Why were you there?"

"She wants me to find her husband."

He seemed surprised. "Are you shitting me?"

"No," I said. "Why would I?"

"What makes you think you can find him?"

I shrugged. "Not sure I can. Not sure I am even going to try. I haven't committed to anything yet."

His cellphone buzzed in his pocket. He pulled it out, looked at it, and muttered. He did not look happy.

I pointed at the phone. "Duty calling?"

"Wife," he said. "She can wait."

"Don't make her wait on my account," I said. "I can't help you with Donny Blackmon. I don't know anything."

"You angling for the reward?" The Fraternal Order of Police and a dozen other civic groups had pooled together a reward for information leading to the arrest and conviction of Donny Blackmon. I didn't know what the various rewards currently totaled, but the last time I had looked it had been more than I'd earned at Whiskey River Investigations to date.

"I could surely use the money," I said, "but I told you, I don't know anything. No starting point, nothing that you all haven't been over a million times. And everyone else has a huge head start on this, compared to me. I'm a babe in the woods on this one. Clueless."

He stared at me for several seconds. "I think I believe you," he finally said. "I know you had a good rep around here, before you left the SO." That would be the Mifflin County Sheriff's Office, which I'd left after a shooting incident. A teen murder suspect had aimed a high-powered rifle with a bump stock at me, and I'd shot him in the leg instead of the chest. I'd hit him, and we'd arrested him, but I was a sniper on the county SWAT team, and other officers had a very difficult time believing I had not hit the guy in the chest. Truth was, I'd shot him in the leg on purpose, and my choice had been a risky move that could have allowed him to fire a hundred rounds or so at my fellow officers if he'd gotten past me. It had been a human decision, made by a human brain that was full of a million conflicting impulses in that moment, but it was not a good decision, as far as most cops were concerned. I, too, think I screwed that one up.

Anyway, I'm on my own now, and if I make mistakes, I'm the only one who will pay. Theoretically.

"Some of those officers still talk to me," I said. "Some don't."

"If you go looking for Blackmon, I'd like to know," Lannigan said. His phone buzzed in his hand. He glanced at it, then ignored it. Judging by his scowl, it was his wife again.

"Gullick was one of ours, and I liked him," he said. "He treated me good, you know, welcomed the new guy. I want to be the one to bring his killer in. I mean, we all appreciate all the help. We really do. But . . . Gullick was our guy. We want to bring Blackmon in. I want to bring him in. You get that, right?"

"I can certainly understand that," I answered. "Sure, I can keep you posted."

If I went looking for Blackmon, of course, it would be at the behest of a client, and so there were likely to be some things I'd decide not to share with the police—but I saw no need to tell that to Lannigan.

"OK, thanks. I'd appreciate that." He opened the SUV and climbed in. He tossed the buzzing phone onto the seat beside him, and scowled when he did it. Marriages and cops don't always go together well. Maybe Lannigan wasn't too happy about the move to the boondocks. None of my business, though.

Lannigan looked out over the water. "Weird place for a run."

"But I get to see herons," I said.

He glanced at me as if I were mustard on a white shirt. "Keep me posted." Then he fired up the vehicle and drove away.

I grabbed two boxes of books from the trailer. Paperback crime thrillers, mostly, and not the best ones. All of the John D. MacDonalds and Raymond Chandlers and such were already at the farm, filling shelves in the room Linda and I set up as my office for Whiskey River Investigations. While I did the menial labor of loading boxes into the truck, I replayed the discussion with Lannigan in my mind. I kept seeing the sharp green eyes and hearing the undercurrent of menace in his voice. I kept picturing a heron, hovering over a bluegill.

I decided Jim Lannigan really wanted to find Donny Blackmon, but not to arrest him. If Lannigan got there first, Donny Blackmon was likely to get roughed up, possibly killed, for "resisting arrest."

There probably were a lot of other cops who felt exactly the same way.

I imagined myself talking to Donny's daughter. "Sorry, kid. Some angry cops found your daddy before I did. They said he resisted arrest. He got beat up pretty bad. He didn't make it."

Fuck.

I looked at my phone. One message had been entered at my company website. It was vague. "I need help desperate please call." That was all it said, along with a name, Bev, and a phone number.

I called it, and a woman answered. She sounded suspicious.

"Who is this?"

"My name is Ed Runyon, from Whiskey River Investigations. You left a message on my website, looking for help. What seems to be going on?"

"Oh, Mr. Runyon, thank God you called. I can't find any help anywhere and I have tried the police and the sheriff and the FBI and they all tell me they can't—"

"Ma'am, please, slow down a bit. Are you Bev?"

"Yes, Beverly Holsinger. Call me Bev."

"OK. I'm Ed. What is going on?"

"I need to know if my butcher is giving me human meat."

I blinked. "I'm sorry, I think I misheard. Can you repeat that?"

"My butcher is giving me human meat . . . I am sure of it. But I need proof."

I think I blinked five more times. "Human meat? From your butcher?"

"Yes! I can taste the difference. I have gotten the ground beef from them for years, and now it tastes totally different. I am sure they are giving me human meat."

"Bev, I am very sorry, but I will not be able to take your case. Have you reported them to the local health department?"

She coughed. "Yes. They said they would look into it. But they haven't done a damned thing so far."

"Call them back, tell them your beef tastes very different from how it did before, tell them it tastes funky now, you are sure something is wrong. Get them to do an inspection. I am not qualified, honestly, to determine what kind of meat they are—"

"No one wants to help me!"

"Bev, I am sorry, but I've given you the best advice I can, and the truth is, I have a case right now and I do not have time to take on another."

"Well, you useless son of a bitch, you are just like the—"

"Goodbye, Bev."

I ended the call, and looked up at the sky. There was a red-tailed hawk, circling, hunting.

I was going to go hunting, too. I realized I had just made my commitment.

I called Amy Blackmon, and she answered right away. "Yes, Mr. Runyon."

"Call me Ed, please. And I'm going to try to find your husband."

"I'll write the letter now. Thank you. God bless you, sir."

CHAPTER EIGHT

I PICKED UP the letter, mercifully without encountering Cassie. I was still pretty conflicted about all this, and did not want another tug on my heartstrings. Amy Blackmon's tears had been bad enough.

I threw some Bill Monroe into the CD player and tried to feel upbeat. It did not quite work.

When I got to the farm, Linda was on the back deck on the porch swing. She was sipping more lemonade and watching a woodpecker dart back and forth between the oaks and the suet cage hanging from a shepherd's hook behind the house.

"Nice run?"

"Yeah," I said, giving her a kiss. "And I stink, so I am going to go shower, and then I'll be in the office."

"You are taking the case?" Her eyebrows arched and she had a bit of a grin she was trying to hide.

"Yes, I am." I watched the woodpecker—the big one, with the brilliant red head, not the smaller one who shows up less often—and continued. "I met a cop today, and I am pretty sure the cop wants to hurt Donny Blackmon real bad. Maybe Donny deserves that, I don't know. But, I guess, the little girl deserves a chance to see her dad before, well, you know." I pulled the sealed envelope from my pocket. "Letter from Amy to Donny. For his eyes only. So he'll believe me when I find him, and maybe not shoot me."

"I knew you'd take this one. Kiss me."

I did.

"I smell like I just ran around a muddy pond," I said, "because I did. Saw a heron, by the way."

"Ooooh, picture?"

"Nope. I don't run with a phone or camera in hand."

She nodded. "Makes sense. I'll go hiking over there when I get a chance. Maybe I'll see it."

"Good luck. He did not find a fish—at least not while I was there. But I know there are fish in there. I am off to the shower."

Once I no longer smelled like a pig farm, I went upstairs and into the office and opened the fridge. Commodore Perry India Pale Ale, my standard. Then I sat in the recliner, kicked up my feet, and drank while I thought. Directly across from me on the wall was a framed bit of sculpture Linda had created out of the busted wood and strings from my old Martin guitar, which I'd shattered in a dark moment in darker days, when a missing girl case had made the universe seem like somewhere I no longer wanted to be. Those days, I hoped, were behind me, so I decided not to dwell on them. And if you find yourself in such a dark place, for God's sake, lean on the people who love you and get some help. Trust me on that.

I took a deep breath and tried to get back on track. I had accepted a mission. It was time to focus on that.

I took a sip of ale and closed my eyes, envisioning Donny Blackmon. Things had gotten bad for him, and he'd bolted. He was an animal, fleeing a forest fire.

So . . . what would he need? Like all animals—and that's all we humans are, really, even if we've learned to write books and play guitars—he'd need food, water, and shelter. Those were the basics. He'd fled without money, by all accounts. Amy had found his wallet and credit cards in his desk drawer. So he'd have to hole up somewhere where he could meet those basic needs.

I tried to put myself in his place. Where would I go if I was broke, and needed shelter and food?

I had not seen any deer heads or bear heads mounted on walls in the Blackmon home and, supposedly, he had not grabbed any guns when he ran, although he had so many that, frankly, I'm not so certain Amy would have noticed if one was missing. I had not seen any bows or arrows or archery targets at the Blackmon home. I would ask Amy about it, but at first glance, it did not seem Donny was equipped to live in the backcountry when he fled. Most likely, he was not doing the Robin Hood thing and hiding in the forest and feasting on the king's deer. So, where would he go?

I had no reason to believe he'd seek help from family or friends, even if they were in another state. Police would check all of those possibilities. Indeed, I'd seen multiple news accounts of interviews with friends and relatives of Donny Blackmon, all swearing up and down they had not seen him. Most of those same stories reported that police had interviewed those same people and, in some instances, even conducted searches. It was a safe bet most, if not all, of those people were still under surveillance. Police officers will volunteer for unpaid overtime if they are seeking a cop killer.

I tried to put myself in Donny's place. I decided if I had been on the run, no money, no gun, no bow, no fishing rod—I'd seek out a church. Churches are pretty damned good places to find help. They feed people, they clothe people. Sometimes they even shelter people. A lot of people in trouble could do way worse than seeking help at a church. Hell, I'd ended up at a church myself years back when I was at the lowest point in my life. I never signed up for all of the creeds and doctrine, but I appreciated the help I got and I met some great people. It had been a good step for me.

It seemed a likely step for Donny Blackmon. He often talked about God and the Bible on his blog.

I grabbed my iPad from the side table and did a quick Google search for free community meals in Ohio. There were hundreds. The cities—Columbus, Cleveland, Akron, Toledo, etcetera—each had dozens. Small-town churches offered meals, too. A man who kept moving near one of the cities might find a meal or two every day, enough to fend off starvation.

I did some mental calculations and estimated there were eleventy-seven bazillion churches in Ohio that Donny could have picked. Jodyville, a tiny place with just one traffic light and about 600 people, had three churches. And I wasn't even sure Blackmon had stayed in the Buckeye State. Hell, he could have run to Kentucky. Or Florida. Or the Rockies. He could be sitting on top of a mountain in Tibet, smoking cigars with a Sherpa. How the fuck was I supposed to find this guy?

I had no way to narrow things down.

I remembered that Donny's blog, the *Blackmon Report*, was pretty thick with Bible references. Donny wrote about Jesus almost as much as he did about guns. He seemed to know more about weaponry than he knew about Christ, but he asserted to his dear readers that he was truly devoted to both.

I looked up his blog. I paused when I saw his picture. A burly guy, with a black beard and dark hair beneath a John Deere cap. I tried to imagine him with a clean-shaven face, or with a full-on wizard beard. I envisioned him with a shaven pate, or a new hair color. I decided to focus on some aspect that would be more difficult to change, and decided on the shape of his nose. It likely had been broken at least once in his life, and seemed to slope in a slightly off-kilter way.

I stared at that nose until I was sure I could recognize it again, no matter what kind of hair or what color of eyes surrounded it. Then I scrolled past a few things about how evil liberals are and hit the search function. I searched for "Bible."

The first thing I hit, in a post about a revolver Donny loved, believe it or not, was a reference to Hebrews 13:2: "Do not neglect to show hospitality to strangers, for thereby some have entertained angels unawares." My first thought was that *Angels Unawares* might be a pretty damned good name for a detective novel if I ever decided to stop being a detective and start writing about fictional detectives instead. My second thought was that a stranger who showed up at Blackmon's house was more likely to be greeted with a gun in the face than with a plate full of warm chocolate chip cookies. I've had both of those happen to me, and I'll take the cookies every time.

I spent a half hour or so scrolling through blog posts and comments. I did not hit upon any obvious pastors inviting Donny to visit or references to specific churches or anything else that would make my job easier. I shut down the iPad and went to grab another beer.

Once I was back in the recliner, I tried a little meditation. Yeah, I know. You're supposed to sit on the floor when you do that, with your legs tied up in a pretzel. And you're not supposed to drink when you do it, either. But I like to improvise, and I'm not a Buddhist, anyway. Tuck says the important thing about meditation is what goes on between your ears, not how you sit. I don't know if he is right or wrong about that, but he's the closest thing I have to a spiritual leader, so what the hell.

I took a sip of beer. I leaned back in the recliner and put up my feet. I closed my eyes. I tried to put myself in Donny's position. What would I do?

Holed up, afraid to be seen, hiding from the world because every cop in the nation wanted to blow him away. So worried about all this that he had not even told his wife and child where he'd gone. Hadn't even tried to contact them since bolting. Hell, he'd left them with no option but to hire a fledgling private eye just to find him and let him know his little girl was dying.

What could possibly draw a guy so paranoid out of whatever hidey-hole he'd found?

My phone buzzed, and I opened my eyes. The first thing I saw was Linda's sculpture mounted on the wall, a Picasso rearrangement of the Martin guitar I'd destroyed in a dark moment.

Donny Blackmon played guitar. He jammed with other musicians. He owned several nice guitars, including a precious one signed by one of the best flat-pickers ever, Tony Rice.

Music was in Donny Blackmon's veins. It was food and life to him. Lonely, scared, on the run—he'd try to find music. Somewhere, somehow.

That's what I would do.

My phone buzzed again, so I stopped looking at Linda's artwork and checked my messages.

Someone had visited the Whiskey River Investigations website. Usually, that meant some woman thought her husband was cheating, or somebody thought the CIA was hacking their flat-screen TV. The new inquiry, though, had nothing to do with spyware or husbands who can't keep it zipped up.

The new message was a threat.

"If you go after Donny, I will fucking kill you!"

I put the phone down, and took another swig of beer.

OK. So . . . I was going to have to keep my eyes open when I went looking for Donny.

Ain't life grand?

CHAPTER NINE

I HEADED DOWNSTAIRS, trying to decide whether or not to tell Linda about the threatening message. I didn't want to worry her, but I didn't want to keep her in the dark, either. Relationships are complicated. I'd had one once where I followed a woman to New York only to have her end up sleeping with a lawyer who made way more money than I did and who probably was easier to get along with. So, I don't pretend to know what I am doing where relationships are concerned.

I found Linda on the back deck, grilling hamburgers and sweet corn. The corn was foil-wrapped, with butter and jalapeños tucked in with it. The aroma climbed into my head and made my belly rumble.

"That's way more food than we can eat, but I'll do my best," I said.

She looked at me and smiled. "Sorry, love. It's not all for you. We need to feed our company."

"I think Lana is a vegan, and I believe Shelly supports her by not eating meat when they are together."

Linda glared at me. "That is some first-class bullshit, Mr. Runyon. I've seen Shelly go berserker on beef tacos while Lana sipped margaritas and watched. Don't worry. You'll get more than enough beef even if we deign to share."

I sighed. "It was worth a try. When are they getting here?"

"Soon."

I took a whiff of all the good aromas coming from the grill. "I'll slice some tomatoes and onions. And I'll dig out the Amish cheddar."

"Good call. I made sangria. Oh, and I told Tuck, too. He's coming by a bit later. Did you figure out some way to track down Cassie's dad?"

I nodded. "I think I have the glimmer of a hint of a ghost of an idea."

"That's more than you had before, right?"

"Yep."

"Then good job." She gave me a quick kiss and then started flipping burgers.

I headed to the kitchen. I decided I could bounce some ideas off of Shelly, a damned good cop, before telling Linda that someone had threatened to kill me if I looked for Donny Blackmon. I wondered if accountants or real estate agents had to deal with such things. I doubted it. I also doubted I could change my line of work right away. I'm bad with numbers, and the only thing I know about real estate is that I don't want to deal with neighbors.

By the time our guests had climbed out of Shelly's Mazda, Linda had the burgers and fixings all arranged on the table on the screened-in portion of the back deck. She'd made a pitcher of sangria and found some cookies that I'm guessing she'd been hiding from me. Linda ran out for hugs, and there was a multicolored swirl of hair in the wind—Shelly's dark, Lana's blonde, and Linda's red. Lots of smiles and hugs set against a backdrop of growing corn and woods beyond. The scene should have been captured for a postcard or a commercial.

After the women separated, I got my hugs, too. I even got some kisses on the cheek.

"How are you, Ed?"

"Hungry, Shelly. We've got a feast out back. Did you bring me a copy of your grisly horror novel?"

"Yeah, all printed out for you. I know you hate reading from a screen."

"Can't wait to read it."

She smiled. Shelly's smiles are electric. "Yeah, can't wait to become a famous horror author and sell the movie rights and live a life of luxury where I don't have to deal with perps."

I leaned close. "Funny you should mention that," I whispered.

She looked concerned. "What the fuck are you into now?"

Linda and Lana were ahead of us by a few yards, arm in arm. "I'll tell you when I get a chance. I want to pick your brain. Are you two staying over tonight? We have room."

"We have a hotel reservation in Port Clinton, so just a drop-by for a few hours. Sorry about the short notice. Planets just kind of lined up for us, other plans got canceled, and we decided to go have some fun."

"Good for you. We'll take a little walk later."

* * *

Tuck swallowed a bite of sweet corn, and glanced at Shelly. "You don't mind if I read your book, too, do you?"

Shelly seemed surprised. "You're a poet. My book is all blood splatters and internal organs suddenly becoming external," she said.

Tuck grinned. "Good. I love horror books. Great way to exorcise your own demons, right? Some cathartic fictional bloodshed never hurt anyone."

"OK," Shelly said. "You can read it."

"Can you email me a copy? I don't want to wait on Ed to finish. Dude reads slower than a lecture on social mores among the Amish."

"Sure," Shelly answered. "It's not Stephen King or anything, I should warn you."

"That is fine," Tuck said. "We already have a Stephen King, anyway."

I stood up. "Not to interrupt this fascinating discussion of disemboweled people and my slow reading pace, but I want to ask Shelly some questions about my case. Cop stuff."

"Go ahead," Linda said. "I want to hear it, too. Sounds interesting."

"I'd rather not talk about the details in a crowd," I said.

Lana and Shelly exchanged glances, and Lana seemed to pick up on some kind of signal. "Guys, I can tell you about some of my wastrel adventures from yesteryear while the cop and the ex-cop go discuss stakeouts or informers or, hell, I don't know. Enhanced interrogation techniques."

"I don't torture people," Shelly said, leaning over and kissing Lana. "Unless we're playing, of course."

Tuck's eyes widened. "Well. Um. I think I want to hear about some wastrel adventures."

Lana grinned at him. "Well, then. I have some wild parties to tell you about. And some wilder after-parties."

I took Shelly by the hand, and we walked away. A glance back showed me both Tuck and Linda seemed enthralled by whatever Lana was telling them.

"Your girl seemed to know we needed to talk in private."

"Yeah," Shelly said. "She is quite intuitive. So, what's going on, cowboy?"

We topped a slight rise in the backyard and headed down toward the barn. Now we were completely out of sight. I told her about the

Blackmon case—and I could skip a lot of details, because every cop in Ohio was intimately familiar with what had happened to Officer Brandon Gullick—and about Cassie's medical situation. I told her about my conversation with Lannigan, the angry cop. Then I told her about the threat sent via my website.

"Damn," she said. "Have you tried to trace that?"

"Not yet," I replied. "But you and I both know it is almost certainly going to go back to some anonymous texting app or a VPN or something. Only the dumbest of dumbasses would have sent me a threat like that using his own number or IP address. I'll check, of course, but . . . you know."

She nodded. "Yeah. Probably. So, who would want you to stay away from Donny Blackmon?"

I started pacing. "No idea. But the universe of people who know I'm looking for Donny has to be pretty damned small. Right? Amy Blackmon, of course, and her daughter. Linda, Tuck, Lana, and you. And, of course, probably every cop and deputy in Mifflin County. They were watching the Blackmon farm. Lannigan was on me pretty quick. I assume word has gotten around."

Shelly's forehead furrowed. "Why would any cop not want you to find Donny?"

I shrugged. "I don't know."

"They want him found, right?"

"Oh, hell yeah."

She shrugged, too. "So, why wave you off?"

"I don't know. Maybe because they'd rather find him themselves so they can do some intense, enhanced interrogation."

Her face went a bit dark. "You think cops want to find him and kill him."

"Stranger things have happened."

Shelly started pacing, too. She then stopped and looked out across the cornfield. Beyond, a hill of oaks rose, and beyond that, blue sky and clouds. "You know, you'd think a man living out here in the fucking Shire would have a slightly brighter view of humanity."

"They think he killed a cop, Shelly."

"I think he killed a cop, too, Ed, but, damn." Her eyes fired up. "You know damn well I could keep that shit in check and bring this guy in. So could almost every cop I know."

I raised a finger, like a professor making a point. "You said *almost*, Shelly, implying you recognize that there are some cops who would not do the job as professionally as you."

"Well, some, maybe, but—"

I interrupted. "And how many bad cops would it take to kill one Donny Blackmon?"

"I see your point." She looked like she wanted to punch me, but she inhaled deeply and calmed down.

"Still doesn't make sense, though, for a cop to threaten you like that."

"Maybe. I'm having a tough time thinking of anyone else with a motive, though."

"Donny got friends who might try to chase you off? Somebody who doesn't want him found?"

"Possibly. I'm going to go talk to a guy tomorrow." I told her about Blackmon's connections among local musicians and how I thought that might give me an inroad to finding him.

"Now you are making some sense, cowboy." Shelly nodded, and smiled. "All those concerts and festivals that got canceled over the damned pandemic, that's a long time to go without live music, if that's your thing. Sure. I see it. Lonely guy, hiding from everyone.

He might take a chance to see a show. They have festivals for that kind of thing, right?"

"Yeah," I said. "I've been to a few. Band after band throughout the day, lots of campfires and pickers all night. It's a good time."

"Hillbilly music, though, right?"

I laughed. "Yeah."

"Not my bag. But I do think you might be onto something."

"Me, too."

We started walking toward the house. "Don't forget that message, though. Sometimes they just want to scare you, but . . ."

"Sometimes they have big guns and lots of bullets," I said. "Do you think I should tell Linda about that?"

Shelly looked at me. "The message? Why shouldn't you?"

I shrugged. "It's most likely just bullshit, you know? Why worry her about something that is bullshit?"

"If it was me, I'd tell Lana," she said. She folded her arms across her chest and gave me a big dose of attitude.

"You would?"

She sighed. "Yes. I know it would cause her some worry, but I also know she's a strong person and, honestly, when I tell her shit, she usually has smart advice. Or hugs or kisses or foot rubs or whatever it is I need. But I don't keep shit from her because, hell, she'd probably know if I was. It's part of why I love her."

I laughed. "Maybe you're right. Lana seems very perceptive."

"Linda is strong and perceptive, too, cowboy. Tell her about it. Tell her it may be nothing, probably is nothing, probably it's every bit as empty as all the other anonymous threats a cop gets. But tell her."

"Will do. Thanks."

When we got back to the table, everyone was red-faced and laughing.

Tuck was the first to regain the ability to speak. "Ed, get Lana to tell you how she saw Ryan Reynolds naked!"

Lana tried to speak, and fought for coherence. "Not Ryan! His . . . his . . . stand-in!" She tilted her head forward until it touched the table, and laughed so hard it rattled ice cubes in the pitcher. There was very little sangria left in the pitcher.

"A stand-in is close enough," Linda said, arching her eyebrows, taking a sip, and turning her head away.

I was indignant. "You'd leave me for a fake Ryan Reynolds?"

She drained her glass. "Only for a week or so. Then I'd come back. I'd miss your chili."

Lana bellowed.

I looked at Shelly. "You're driving, right?"

She sighed. "I am now."

Later that night, just as I'd been about to tell Linda about the weird threatening message, she'd taken the discussion in a different direction. She'd grabbed my hand, pulled me toward the bedroom, and told me to convince her not to leave me for a faux Ryan Reynolds.

I did my best.

CHAPTER TEN

LINDA OWNS A few Maxfield Parrish prints. They are notable for cotton-candy clouds, tinted with hints of rainbows around the edges. Early the next morning, I was driving beneath just such a sky. I love Ohio.

I stopped at the Mifflin County Sheriff's Office to get copies of investigation reports concerning the death of Officer Brandon Gullick. The woman in records wore a name badge on a cord around her neck that said her name was Amanda Clayton. I did not know her, but she seemed to know who I was. Not that she gave me a dirty look or anything, but she did not ask my name or my interest in the Gullick case. Her face was very neutral, professionally so.

I noted she made a hushed phone call from a desk far away from the window before coming back and telling me to take a seat while she processed my request. That's fancy cop lingo for "print your documents."

I nodded.

I chose a rather ugly seat next to a cheap side table and sat down, then took a sip of coffee from my Thermos. I had known I'd be waiting a little while, so I had come prepared.

There were neither magazines nor newspapers to help citizens wile away their time while they wait, so I just sat and thought. None of my thoughts were particularly productive.

After fifteen minutes or so, the outer door opened to admit a tall and wiry fellow with long, limp hair and a long, limp cigarette. He wore a blue button-up shirt with a long, limp black tie. He strode to the service window and said hello.

Officer Clayton did not leave her desk. "There is an ash container outside, sir. Extinguish your cigarette there."

He grinned, with the smoke clenched in his teeth, and spoke through the cloud it produced. "Just us, right? I'll only be a minute."

Her eyebrows lifted. "Out." She went back to work and ignored him.

The newcomer stared at her for a moment, shrugged, then turned. In doing so, he noticed me. "It's a nanny state," he said.

"There's a very clear sign on the door. Maybe you missed it on the way in."

He grinned and exhaled a bank of fog worthy of a werewolf movie. "Must have."

He stepped outside, walked past the ash container, and hurled his cigarette into the parking lot, then came back in. He went straight to the window and told the woman, "I'm Jerry Spence, a private investigator out of Columbus. I wanted to talk to Detective Scott Baxter about updates in the search for Donny Blackmon. I met here with Baxter a couple times on this already. He knows me."

She shook her head. "This is records. I have no idea whether Detective Baxter is available to speak to you or not. I suggest you call him to make arrangements, or if you are in a hurry you can enquire at dispatch. Walk out of this office and turn right. The next door down is the one you want."

I noted how she regarded Spence with the same detached manner she'd given me, and how she'd rebuffed him twice now in a totally professional way. Records clerks deal with people all day long every day, and she seemed to have decided the best way to cope was to treat them all with cool neutrality.

Spence winked. "OK, yeah. I guess I got the wrong office. Sorry. Should have kept my smoke, I guess, huh?"

Officer Clayton ignored that and went back to work. "Have a good day, sir."

Spence turned toward the exit, then paused when he saw me. "I think I know you," he said.

"Can't say the same," I replied.

He wagged a finger at me. "You shot up the football star a while back, right? Runyon?"

"The football star tried to shoot me, too," I answered.

He grinned. "I knew it." He crossed the space between us and held out his hand. "Jerry Spence, private investigator. I read you went into the PI game, too?"

His grip was strong, even though his limbs were thin compared to mine. His eyes were shiny, almost glassy. I'd have suspected marijuana in the cigarette he'd tossed, but I didn't smell any.

"Yeah," I said. "I'm giving it a try."

He leaned closer and adopted a conspiratorial tone. "You looking for Donny Blackmon?"

I decided not to answer that. "I guess you are, since you asked about it."

He stared at me a moment, exhaled sharply, and stood up straight. "So that's how it is, huh? No info sharing? No reciprocals?"

I shrugged. "I very seldom discuss business with someone I met randomly twenty seconds ago."

He grinned. "Sure. Well. Be seeing you."

Spence walked out. He went straight to a late-model Toyota sedan—gray, nondescript, good choice if you don't want to stand out in traffic—and climbed in. I watched him pull out, then Officer Clayton appeared at the window. "Mr. Runyon? Your documents are ready."

CHAPTER ELEVEN

I DID NOT look at the MCSO reports right away. I could do that anytime, for instance, late at night when normal people were sound asleep. Instead, I aimed my F-150 for Henry Road in search of Tug Burrell's place in Ambletown, a city of about twenty thousand people that was the center of everything in Mifflin County. I wanted to ask him about playing music with Donny Blackmon.

It was a nice morning, and a brief hard rain had cooled things down. Drops still fell from oak branches, and the climbing heat drew ghosts of steam up from the pavement. The cool respite wasn't likely to last a long time.

I had not called ahead because Burrell had an unlisted number, and Amy Blackmon did not have it. So, I was depending on dumb luck.

I heard some familiar banjo licks as I rounded the corner and saw the double-wide trailer I was seeking. A John Hartford tune, "Steam-Powered Aereo Plane." No one was singing, and there was no accompaniment, so the player was improvising quite a bit. It sounded pretty good. The song had been recorded by dozens of people, and this player seemed to be incorporating bits of all those interpretations into his own thing.

Tug Burrell kept playing even as I pulled into the long driveway and walked up to the trailer, set back far from the road and surrounded by tall grass that needed cutting. He was twice as fat as the typical fat man and had twice as much beard as Santa Claus, except his was dark red. He sat on a large, weather-worn deck that leaned a bit to the north. He spat a brown wad of tobacco into the tall grass and gave me a brief nod to acknowledge my existence. But he kept playing his battered Deering, and his talent was evident.

I just listened until he was done. "Sounded really good," I said. "Tough song to play."

He grinned widely. "You a music critic?"

"No," I said. "Private investigator."

His face darkened immediately. "No comment."

"I understand your hesitation," I said. "You are Donny Blackmon's friend and everyone thinks he's a murderer. Would it help any if I told you I was working for his wife?"

He spat again. "Might," he said. "If you can prove it."

"Call her," I said. "I have her number if you don't."

Burrell stared at me for a few moments, then placed his banjo on the stand next to him. "You don't sound like you are lying," he said. "Want a beer?"

I stepped up and sat on a lawn chair across from him. "No thanks. Amy tells me you pick with her husband."

"Yeah, now and then." He spat again, and now that I was closer, I could tell his left cheek was way fatter than the right one, because it was full of tobacco. "Been a while, though. Too long."

"I am sure he feels the same way," I replied.

Burrell fixed me with a hard stare. "If you're asking did he call me or anything and say 'Hey, let's get together and jam,' the answer is no. Donny is laying low, and he's not dumb enough to do that."

"I don't suppose he is," I said. "But his wife wants me to get a message to him, and, well, I'm going to try to do that."

"What kind of message?"

I sighed. "I'll let Amy Blackmon decide who she's going to tell. Her business, not mine."

"It's about her little girl," Burrell said.

I kept a poker face.

"Well," he said, "I can respect you keep her privacy and all. OK. But I don't know nothing. That I swear."

"Fair enough," I said. "Who else did you and Donny pick with?"

He looked at me like I was a half-cleaned fish someone had dumped on his lap. Then he grinned. "Well, you been fair with me so I reckon you'll be fair with them. We go by Turkey Gravy Boys." He laughed. "Hard to find a name ain't been used. Stan Blake, he lives in Jodyville and plays mandolin. Charley Getts plays guitar, but he's over in Wooster and works pretty weird hours. He practices on his own and then meets up with us when he can, but he's real good and it don't hurt us much. Bob Russett plays the doghouse bass and he is in Ambletown. Sings pretty good, too, but . . ."

"But what?"

Burrell spat again, beating his previous best distance by a yard. "Bobby and Donny both hate cops something fierce," he said. "I don't go that way, you know. I treat every person like a person and give them a chance to do me wrong or do me right, then I react accordingly, you know? But Bobby? He's likely to see a private whatever as just another cop, and the last batch that came to tell him to turn his damned music down got greeted with a gun. No shots fired, and his wife calmed him down, but he drew on them."

"Duly noted. Is he a drinker?"

Burrell laughed. "Who around here ain't these days?"

I nodded. "Is he a day drinker? I'm just trying to decide when to show up. I'd prefer not to get shot."

"Nah, he don't drink that much," Burrell said. "But go early rather than late, I'd say."

"Do you have any idea where Donny might have run to?"

"Wish I did."

I pointed at the Deering. "You play good. I just strum chords on a guitar and sing a little."

He nodded. "Thanks. Tuning up for a gig. Mud Run Bluegrass Festival. Down in Pike County. Ain't played live in a while, goddamned COVID. Got to get my chops back up."

"Amy says Donny didn't play gigs with you guys."

He shook his head. "He helped us out a few times when Charley got stuck working, but no, Donny just wants to pick, you know? Around a campfire, playing easy stuff, that is OK now and then, but for him it is mostly about playing really tough stuff and seeing if he can get it right. Like Doc Watson tunes. He'd rather pick something tough and make us stop at the same damn measure ten times in a row until he gets it right. You know? Can't do that onstage in front of a crowd, but you can do it if you are just jamming, or sitting out back with family. Donny is odd that way. Real good picker, though. I mean he can hit Doc's licks more often than not. I love playing with him."

I took one of my cards out of my wallet and dropped it into the open banjo case next to him. "If you hear from Donny, or think of anything that might help me find him, please give me a call. It's important. You'll be doing his family a favor."

He nodded. "If it seems right, I will."

"Thanks for your time."

I walked back to my truck, and the sad tune of "Wayfaring Stranger" filled the air at my back. By the time I reached the truck,

I was singing softly. "I'm just a poor wayfaring stranger, traveling through this world below."

Donny Blackmon was a wayfaring stranger. But where was he?

I checked my phone before pulling out of the driveway. There were no new messages threatening to slit my throat or blow out my brains if I kept up my search for Donny Blackmon. I still hadn't mentioned that threat to Linda. I started to call her, but I knew she was busy, and it seemed the sort of discussion we should have in person. So, I looked up Bob Russett's address and headed that way. I figured maybe I could catch him with a hangover. That would give me the edge.

CHAPTER TWELVE

Bob Russett wasn't hungover, but he was coughing and sneezing in a horrible way.

I'd found his house and his wife had told me he was a construction worker, building a barn out on Paradise Hill. It was a pole barn, about halfway done, and when finished it probably would be able to house four tractor-trailers with ease. Bob was on the roof when I arrived, but a nice guy named Roy waved him down for me. Russett coughed hard as he approached, and I backed up. I pulled my mask out of my pocket and put it on.

"It ain't COVID," he said, sneering through his gray beard. He reminded me of Jerry Seinfeld a bit. He seemed perpetually surprised, and like he was trying not to laugh at some joke.

I held up a hand, and he stopped about ten feet from me. "COVID or not, I don't want it."

"It ain't COVID," he repeated. "That's all bullshit."

I decided to avoid a lengthy debate and just got straight to the point. "I'm looking for Donny Blackmon. You play music with him sometimes, I hear."

"So?"

"So, I'm wondering if you've heard from him, or have some thoughts on where he might be."

"I haven't, and I don't." He turned his back to me and headed toward the ladder he'd used to descend. "I got work to do."

"So do I," I said. "Donny's wife wants me to find him."

He waved a hand in the air without looking back. "Sure she does."

I watched Russett climb all the way up and kept watching until he'd driven three more nails. Then I got in my truck and left.

CHAPTER THIRTEEN

DETECTIVE SCOTT BAXTER had agreed to have lunch with me, and he was already at a window-side table at Whitey's Diner when I showed up. He was wearing a blue polo shirt and seemed to have added some muscles on his thin frame since the last time I'd seen him. He still looked more like a young minister than a cop, and he'd probably have a Mayberry vibe his whole life. I knew for a fact he was a good wrestler, though. High school legend, and many local athletic departments had tried to hire him as a coach. He loves being a cop, though, and he loves it more now that he's a detective.

My departure from the Mifflin County Sheriff's Office had paved the way for that promotion, by the way. I feel good about that.

"How are you, Ed? Fine as frog's hair, I hope?"

"Something like that. Thanks for meeting with me. I'm buying."

"I'll let you," he said. "And I'm having pie for dessert, so be warned."

"Duly noted."

We chatted until our coffees showed up, black for me and cream and sugar for Bax. Then he winked at me. "This is about the Blackmon hunt, ain't it?"

"You are sharper than people think," I answered.

He chuckled. "We keep that place under close watch," he said. "I saw some very nice drone video of your truck pulling into the Blackmon driveway, you know. Saw you walk back to the barn with Amy and have a look, too."

"Well, I wasn't trying to sneak, you know."

"Yeah." He took a sip of coffee, then smiled as our food arrived. Fried chicken and mashed potatoes for him, eggs over easy and hash browns for me, plus a side of sausage. The waitress, maybe all of sixteen, refilled our coffee mugs and asked if we needed anything else. We didn't.

"So what do you need from me, Ed?"

"I'd like to know what's not in the public reports."

Bax took a mouthful of chicken, and closed his eyes. "Like heaven on a stick," he said after swallowing. "So good. Anything specific?"

"You know," I said. "Something you haven't told the press, or let slip in interviews."

He wiped his mouth with a napkin. "You're going for the reward, I reckon."

"Sure. I got bills." I had no reason to tell him about the mission I'd accepted from Amy Blackmon.

"Well," Bax continued. "OK. I guess I can tell you something. I can trust you."

"Of course," I replied.

"Officer Gullick had traces of chloroform, the coroner said." Bax waved a finger around his own nose and mouth. "In the blood. It ain't what killed him, but, well, it was there."

"Someone gassed him?"

Bax nodded his head. "Someone tried, at least. Coroner ain't sure Gullick went under, says it ain't conclusive. But Gullick was hit in the back of the head hard enough to knock him out, and well, ain't no reason to clobber someone if you've chloroformed him, and there ain't no reason to gas him if you've knocked him out, right? I mean, it's like plucking a chicken you already ate." He took another bite of dark meat.

I thought about what Bax had told me. "That sounds more and more like someone deliberately dragged Gullick to Donny's barn and killed him."

Bax took a sip of coffee but said nothing.

I didn't ask why that information about the chloroform had never been made public. Cops always want to have some aces up their sleeve, some details that the general public—and more importantly, potential suspects—don't know the cops have. It gives suspects a chance to trip themselves up.

I lowered my voice. "You don't think Blackmon killed Gullick, do you?"

"It is not a popular opinion, but I do not. Most of the SO just figures Donny did it, case closed."

"But you are not convinced."

"Not really. If you were Donny Blackmon, would you drag a guy to your own property and kill him there? And then leave your own gun behind? And if you were Gullick, would you go up to Donny's property in your running clothes, unarmed? None of that makes sense. I sure as hell want to find Donny Blackmon, though. And, I got to say, running the way he did sure looks guilty."

"Thanks, Bax. Anything else I ought to know?"

"Just search fast if you want the reward. You have a fair amount of competition."

I nodded. "I met one of them. Guy named Spence."

Baxter laughed. "The skinny squirrelly guy, yeah. He's a tool, and I don't mean a sharp one. He's been by the SO to hit me up for updates three times in the last month. I hope he steps in a bear trap."

I laughed. "I didn't think much of him, either, but I wouldn't wish that on him."

Bax shook his head. "I keep telling him, if I knew anything that would help locate Donny Blackmon, I'd just go locate Donny Blackmon myself, but Spence just keeps flapping around like a green buzzard."

I did not ask why the buzzard had to be green, or if buzzards ever actually were green. Nor did I congratulate Bax for not butchering his tool metaphor earlier. Bax is a smart guy, but metaphors just aren't his thing. "Have you talked with the guys Donny played music with?"

"Yeah, they don't know nothing and I believe them when they say it."

"Russett seems very unfriendly."

Bax nodded. "He does not like sworn officers of the law, not one little bit."

"Does he have an alibi for the night Gullick was killed?"

"Not a great one. Says he was home alone, playing a bass. Neighbors say they didn't see him, but they say they heard him playing."

I finished my coffee. "He has a stereo, I presume."

"A real nice one," Bax said. "Nice recording gear, too."

The waitress returned. "Anything else, guys?"

"Nope," I said.

"Banana cream pie," Bax reminded me.

"Oh, right. Make it two."

We talked about other things while we ate our dessert and drank more coffee. But the details of the Blackmon case swarmed in my mind. Big green buzzards.

CHAPTER FOURTEEN

I SPENT THE next three days calling Donny's other musician pals and learning nothing new. I'd called more than two-dozen churches all over Ohio, asking if any newcomers had shown up for free meals or clothing. Plenty of people had done so, of course, because there was need everywhere. But no one had seen anyone who looked anything like Donny Blackmon.

I'd perused the files from the Mifflin County Sheriff's Office, too. Plenty of gory details about Officer Brandon Gullick's death. A statement from his widow, Beth, in which she said she had no idea at all how her husband had gone to a Mifflin County farm and gotten himself murdered. Everyone loved him, she'd said.

That added up with what I'd heard. Gullick was a good guy. Coached a baseball team. Taught self-defense classes. Volunteered with the Christmas toy collection. Good husband, good father, good cop. Everyone agreed.

The cops considered his dead body as rather conclusive evidence that someone, indeed, had not loved Brandon Gullick. They had reviewed his past cases to see if, perhaps, he'd arrested someone who might have had vengeful friends. A brief report signed by MCSO Detective Scott Baxter less than two weeks ago indicated that avenue of investigation had thus far been fruitless.

Speaking of fruitless, I'd also run a check on the phone number used to threaten me and, sure enough, it was registered to a free texting app that let people use fake phone numbers to send messages. With an attorney and a million years, I might be able to use a subpoena to get the service provider to reveal who had sent the threat, but if the threat was serious, I'd be shot or something long before justice prevailed in the courts. And I couldn't afford an attorney right now, anyway. I decided to ignore the threat. People had tried to kill me before.

Given all the dead ends, my mood and attitude were not exactly great, so the ever-vigilant Linda had come up with an idea.

She and I were having a lunch of salami sandwiches and soft drinks by the pond. We'd hoped to spot the heron, but he was not hunting the waters today.

"He knows we want to see him, so he's shy," Linda said.

"Or he's moved on because he didn't get a fish here last time," I countered.

"I know there are fish in there, Ed, because you catch them."

"Yeah, but the heron didn't."

She grinned. "So, you are a better hunter of fish than a heron, whose very survival depends on catching the fish? You can go to Burger King, right? But the heron is adapted to hunt. You are not."

I decided not to argue and kissed her instead.

My phone buzzed before the kiss could lead to anything more amorous and adventurous.

"Another threat?" Linda looked concerned. I'd followed Shelly's advice and told Linda about the previous message. Linda was worried, of course, but she was being brave.

"No," I told her. "It's Tuck. Wants to know if I can call him." I did.

"Hey, Ed, have you seen the news today?"

"Nope. No news, no clues, no herons. I have my lady by my side, though, and a nice sandwich. What's up?"

"A cop got killed in Chillicothe this morning. People are telling reporters they've seen Donny Blackmon around."

"Are you shitting me?"

"Wish I was, Ed. Hate to see anyone get killed. But you are looking for Donny, right?"

"Yeah. OK, thanks, man. I'll check into it."

Linda was all wide-eyed. "Break in the case?"

"Maybe. I hope not. Cop got killed, in Chillicothe or thereabouts. People apparently say they've seen Donny around there."

"You going?"

"Yeah, I have to."

She gulped, and tried not to sound too worried. "Be safe, be careful."

"I will."

"Oh, and there is a donut place, Crispy Creme. On Bridge Street, I think. Not the chain that spells both words with a *K*—this place spells both with a *C*. Bring me some of the ones with chocolate frosting and cream filling."

I laughed. "Seriously?"

She nodded. "I was down there a few years ago to see *Tecumseh*," she said, referring to the outdoor drama I'd seen a few times myself, but never with Linda. "And I had some of those donuts. And I want more."

I stood and bowed. "As you wish. And I have a cool date idea. Let's go see an outdoor play full of Shawnee warriors and Simon Kenton and cannons and horses and stuff."

"Sure," she said, lighting up. "When you are done with this case, of course. Oh, and don't get beat up or shot or anything when you go looking for Donny."

"Duly noted."

CHAPTER FIFTEEN

THAT EVENING I was in Chillicothe, Ohio, at a sort-of Irish-styled downtown bar called the Crosskeys Tavern. I was munching on some Reuben egg rolls—like regular egg rolls but stuffed with all the corned beef and kraut and Swiss cheese you'd find on a Reuben sandwich and served with Thousand Island dressing. I was washing it down with an IPA. And I was waiting on a bartender named Aimee to finish making Manhattans for a young couple, so she could come back and tell me about how she had seen Donny Blackmon in her bar a week before Ross County Sheriff's Deputy Ted Klewey had been shot and killed.

Deputy Klewey, according to the same news reports that had led me to Aimee Markham, had pulled over a red Chevy Cavalier for speeding on U.S. 23. He'd been greeted with a bullet in the head from a driver who then bolted like a bat out of hell into the woods, leaving the car behind.

I silently toasted Deputy Klewey and Officer Brandon Gullick and took a deep swig of beer. Cops have a damned tough job, and—especially these days—are not appreciated enough.

The waitress, bleached-blonde-twenties and adorned with three small pieces of metal in her nose and cheeks, waved at me and pointed to a chair at an empty table. "I'll go on break in one minute," she said, making it sound like the most exciting development in the history of humankind. "Talk to you over there!"

I nodded, finished my food, and headed to the table. The place wasn't horribly crowded, and the music was not too loud, though it ran closer to Tuck's metalhead tastes than to my beloved country and folk.

Aimee showed up at the table and placed another cold beer in front of me. "On the house."

I smiled. "And why do I merit this?"

She leaned forward. "Because you are cute as hell and my boyfriend's a jerk."

"I just wanted to talk about the guy you saw in here last week, nothing extracurricular or anything," I said.

"Well, yeah," she replied, sitting up straight. "But you know, things happen." She smiled.

"Not this time, I'm afraid."

She sighed. "Married?"

"Might as well be."

"Well, drink the beer anyway." She laughed. "She's lucky. Anyone ever tell you you look like that actor?"

I took a sip of the free beer. "Heath Ledger?"

"No, not him," she said. "I don't remember the name, or the movie, but you look just like him."

"Miss Markham . . ."

"Aimee. Like the song." She was all business now, the rejected pass forgotten as casually as it had been proffered. Modern romance, I guess.

"OK, Aimee. As I told you earlier, I am a private investigator. You told the reporter from the *Gazette* that you'd seen Donny Blackmon here at the bar last week."

Her eyes widened. They were nice eyes. "Yeah, freakiest thing."

"Tell me about it, please."

She leaned her head to one side. "I think it was Wednesday, maybe Thursday. He came in early, like four or five, and ordered a burger and fries."

"Can you describe him for me?"

"Sure. Dark hair, short beard, black T-shirt, jeans, gray ball cap, nothing on it, no team or company or anything. Big guy, maybe as big as you."

I could tell she'd recited this a couple of times before, and noted it was an almost perfect description of the photo of Donny Blackmon that had been all over the newspapers and Facebook. I would have bet a thousand bucks that Donny did not look like that anymore. If I had a thousand bucks, of course. I didn't.

I took a sip of beer. "Anything else?"

She scrunched up her pretty face. "He smelled bad."

"Did you call police, or anyone, when you saw him?"

"No," she said, shaking her head.

"Why not?"

Aimee shrugged. "I don't know, it's weird. When I saw him, he seemed odd, out of place, you know? But I could not figure where I'd seen him before."

"You mostly get regulars here?"

"New faces aren't totally rare, but yeah, it's a fairly regular crowd mostly, I'd say."

"If you didn't recognize this guy as Donny Blackmon right away, what made you think it was him later?"

She smiled. "You know, it's just weird. I guess it all clicked when that poor policeman got shot. I mean, God, how bad is that? I was like, oh my God, you know? It just clicked, I guess. I remembered seeing about it on Facebook. The cop killer."

We observed a five-second moment of silence, then she continued. "I'd seen that guy, Blackmon, in the news and read about him and all that. So, I had to call the police here, you know?"

"Sure," I said. "This guy who came in, did he talk to anyone else?"

"No, just me. And just to order, you know? No small talk or nothing. Kept to himself."

"Did he pay by credit card or cash?"

"Yeah, cash," she said. "That was weird, too, right? Who carries cash these days? But he did."

"Did you happen to see the vehicle he came in?"

"No, sorry."

"Did you notice which way he went when he left?"

"Didn't really pay attention, sorry. I didn't know who he was then, you know?"

I nodded. "Well, then, thanks for your time, and for the beer. I'm going to leave you with my card, and if you think of anything that might help me find this guy, please give me a call. Anytime."

"Can I call you for any other reason?" She smiled, and her eyebrows arched.

"Sorry. My woman is the jealous type, and she knows where I keep my gun."

She pouted. "Well, nice to meet you, Mr. Runyon."

"You, too."

I was only five steps beyond the door, heading toward a municipal parking lot and my truck, when a man walked up from behind me.

"So, I was right. You are looking for Donny Blackmon."

I turned to glance at the newcomer. "Jerry Spence." He was wearing the same skinny tie I'd seen him wearing before.

"Yeah. I slipped in and sat nearby listening to you talking with the cutie. Surprised you didn't notice me. But I guess you were distracted. She's quite the hottie. You should've taken her up, man."

I kept walking. "Feel free to make your own move, if you like. Is there any point to this conversation?"

"Just, you know, we're both after the same thing—a fat reward. Maybe if we pool our efforts, we have a better chance. We can split it, you know?"

I considered that for a moment. I wasn't eager to have a partner. I'd gone into business for myself expressly so I could take the cases I wanted, handle them my way, and not put anyone else at risk. Also, Spence annoyed me. He seemed clingy, like a Band-Aid. "What, exactly, are you bringing to the table?"

"Well," he said, "I've been on this longer than you. I probably have some stuff you haven't tracked down yet."

"And if that stuff was any good, you wouldn't be chasing me down the street to find out what I knew, would you?"

He stopped walking. I didn't.

"Runyon, I just hear you were a pretty good cop, figured you might have some ins where I don't. That Baxter guy will barely talk to me. You know how cops feel about private investigators, right?"

"I like working alone," I said, still walking. But after five more steps, I stopped and turned, because it occurred to me Spence might know something useful after all. "Did anyone try to chase you off of this case?"

He shrugged. "What do you mean?" He trotted toward me.

"Did you receive any anonymous threats, phone calls, anything like that? Telling you not to go looking for Donny Blackmon?"

"Oh, well, yeah," Spence replied. "I got a weird text message, yeah. I don't take that shit seriously."

"Don't you? What did it say?"

He stared into the night sky. "Uh, let me see, something like don't go looking for Donny Blackmon or you'll regret it. Some shit like that."

"Do you still have the message?"

"Fuck no, I delete shit like that."

"Remember the number it came from?"

"No, man. It was probably fake, anyway."

"OK. Well, be careful. Might just be an idle threat, might be someone who means it."

"You don't want to team up? I mean, safety in numbers, right?"

"No," I said. "I don't want a partner. I like to work by myself, so I can change the plan on the fly if I need to, or not spend time arguing over where to eat."

Spence rubbed his thumb and fingers together. "Think about it, Ed. Lots of money on this. If we double-team this thing, we can be more efficient, right? Half a reward is still pretty good, man. And we can watch each other's backs."

I shook my head. "You've been on this for months, I hear, and you are still chasing down the same shitty leads I am." I started walking away.

"You think that girl was lying?" He caught up to me. "You think she made it up just to, I don't know, get famous or something?"

I sighed. "No, I do not think she is lying. I just think she is wrong. Something bad happened, a cop got killed just doing his job, and like everyone else, she's trying to make sense of it, connect dots, figure out what the hell happened. We humans are pattern-seeking animals, and sometimes we see patterns even if they aren't there. She remembered another Ohio cop got killed, connected this death to that one for no particular reason, and remembered a weird guy she'd seen at the bar last week. I don't know if she accurately described that guy or if she just superimposed Donny Blackmon's photo onto her memory, but I don't think she saw Donny Blackmon."

"I think you are just guessing," Spence said before spitting onto the sidewalk.

"Maybe," I said. "But she didn't recognize Blackmon before this local deputy got killed. And then suddenly she recalls a lot of details that didn't seem to register before. I don't know. Just seems to not be a real lead."

"Maybe. You going to talk to the other people who say they saw Blackmon?"

"Good night, Spence."

I left him standing there. Once I got to my truck, I checked my phone for any new threats. There weren't any.

I got a room at the Holiday Inn out near the highway and called Linda. I told her about my interview with Aimee Markham. "There are two other people who say they saw Donny, and I'm going to check them out in the morning. A truck driver and a pizza delivery kid. Neither of them reported seeing Donny until after this new killing, so my expectations are low."

"You don't think the deaths are related, do you?"

"No, I do not." I stretched out on the bed. "Officer Gullick's killing shows premeditation. Someone got him out to Donny's farm and killed him, and they took a lot of trouble doing so. This new death, it just seems like a random thing, deputy pulls over the wrong guy and gets shot. Sad, but it happens."

I heard Linda's sharp intake of breath. "I'm glad you aren't a cop anymore. Be careful, anyway."

"I will. I love you."

"I love you, too."

I peered out the window, feeling frustrated. When I was a cop, I sometimes felt like I was chasing too many things, a juggler who kept getting extra balls tossed at him until he was forced to drop some of them in order to keep the others going. I'd hoped being a PI would be different and let me work with laser focus. But here I was, chasing down leads that I knew in my heart were probably bullshit, but I was chasing them down anyway because that's what investigators do. Oh, well. At least I wasn't sitting in a sensitivity training class or getting hit with a Taser just so I'd know how perps felt when it happened to them.

Once I decided to go back to work, I tracked down information on the other two people who saw someone they thought was Donny Blackmon, then read the news on the death of Deputy Ted Klewey. He'd left behind a wife, Rachel, and a nine-year-old son, Teddy. Umpired youth baseball games on his days off. Spotless record. And he'd been killed just because he pulled over a speeder. The Cavalier had been stolen from a parking lot in Circleville earlier in the day. The report on that came in about twenty-five minutes after the deputy was murdered.

Meanwhile, the search for the killer continued. U.S. 23 meandered between forested hills. The guy could be hiding anywhere, or he could have easily slipped away.

I don't pray a lot, but I did so that night. I prayed for Deputy Klewey and his family, and for Officer Gullick and his.

And I prayed for justice.

CHAPTER SIXTEEN

THE PIZZA DELIVERY kid who thought he'd seen Donny Blackmon had a second job, cleaning up at a kennel place south of town. He was tossing a small plastic bag of something that smelled foul into a metal container when I found him.

"Are you Joey Barstow?"

"Yeah," he said, turning a hatchet-thin face toward me and blinking.

"I'm Ed Runyon, a private investigator. I understand you believe you saw Donny Blackmon, who is accused of killing a police officer in Mifflin County."

"Oh, yeah," he said, suddenly interested. "I delivered him a pizza."

That detail had not been reported in any of the news accounts I'd seen. "Where did you deliver it?"

"That's the weird part. It was in the park, not at a house or hotel or anything."

I thought about that for a moment. "He called in the order, right? By phone?"

"Yeah," Joey said. "Called and said to deliver it to Yoctangee Park."

"Kind of a big park, isn't it? I drove by it yesterday, I think."

He shrugged. "Yeah, good size, I guess."

"How did you know where to take the pizza?"

"I called him when I was on my way. Met him in the parking lot."

I nodded. "Do you still have his number?"

"Sure," he said, picking up his phone from a fence rail behind the dog poop can. He fumbled around for a few seconds. "Here it is. I gave it to the cops."

I sighed. Donny Blackmon wouldn't even call his wife and kid. No way did he phone in a pizza order.

I knew already it was hopeless, but I dialed the number anyway. A man answered after six rings. "Yeah?"

"Hello, sir. My name is Ed Runyon. I am a private detective. I understand you ordered a pizza—"

"Jesus Christ for the love of God, I already told all of this to the cops! Yes, I ordered a goddamned pizza! Yes, I had it delivered to the park! Yes, it's my business and not yours, so fuck off!"

"Sorry to have troubled you, sir." I ended the call and stared at the pooper scooper. "Well, Joey, I don't think you gave the pizza to a cop killer."

"But it was so weird, you know? And he looked like the guy in the news!"

"My guess is your guy just wanted to order a pizza without his wife finding out, or something like that. He sounds like a grumpy fucker—maybe she kicked him out."

"Really?" He seemed disappointed. "Fuck, man."

"Well, don't worry. Maybe he'll go kill someone and then order another pizza. Thanks for your time."

I walked back to my truck and decided to waste a little more time by calling the truck driver on my list of potential witnesses. I got a recorded message: "This is William Canabaum, and I am on the road, as usual. Leave a message!" That was followed by two toots of a truck horn.

I left a message.

I decided not to call the local sheriff's office or police department. I had no reason at all to think the two cop killings were related. The murder of Brandon Gullick and the search for Donny Blackmon had made national news, and such things always spark a flurry of false reports. People hear something in the news, see something in real life, and then try to make it all connect. It mostly adds up to a waste of time.

I got Linda's donuts and a cup of coffee to go. Once I was on the highway headed north, I turned on some Willie Nelson and ate one of the donuts. I thought about turning around and getting another dozen. It was that good.

Before I reached Columbus, my phone buzzed. It was another threatening text message.

"Stop looking for Donny Blackmon or I kill you. Last warning."

It was from the same number as before.

I spent the rest of the drive randomly changing my speed, taking unnecessary exits, and checking behind me. I was not being followed, as far as I could tell.

With plenty of miles to cover and nothing much to see once I got through Columbus, I started calling a few PIs I knew. Of the five, three had put in some time on the hunt for Donny Blackmon. Two of those had received threats similar to the ones I had received. Neither had taken the threats seriously, and neither had given up hope on the case. But neither had gotten any further than I had, and both had taken on other assignments.

No one had a good idea who might be trying to chase away PIs.

I turned on the music again and thought while I drove. Who might have a motive to make those threats? A friend of Donny's, maybe, who wanted to help him evade capture. Maybe a doghouse bass player who disliked cops as much as Donny did, and who refused to answer my polite questions. I was going to have to try connecting with Bob Russett again.

The *Blackmon Report* was a well-read blog, though, and Russett might not be the only cop hater out there who wished Donny well. The list of potential suspects could be rather long.

Who else had a motive? Maybe a cop, someone who wanted to find Blackmon himself? I remembered Jim Lannigan's hard, determined eyes. I had little doubt that if I shared a lead with him, the Ambletown cop would race pretty hard to find Donny before I did. But would he risk making threats like that? Doubtful. He could hide behind a fake phone number, but in a high-profile case like this one any cop would realize that a subpoena to the fake number provider eventually could get at the evidence.

There was one big consideration in favor of a cop, though. Along with motive, a cop would have opportunity, and by that, I mean a cop might actually have a good idea which private investigators were on the hunt. Blackmon's gun-nut buddies probably would have no real idea. Hmmmm.

CHAPTER SEVENTEEN

"HOW MANY OF my donuts did you eat?" Linda was making a show of not being concerned about the new threat message.

"Just two," I said. "If you don't devour them all, I'd appreciate one for breakfast. That is going to be spectacular with coffee. Hey, it's Friday and I am fresh out of leads. Want to go out tonight?"

"Maybe. I'm kind of midway on my painting, waiting for inspiration." Linda, who loves art as much as she loves books, was working on a landscape. It was a sunset, and she'd gotten the blood-red sun and the gradient sky down on canvas, complete with just enough clouds to catch the rays. She was still fretting over how to get the foreground to properly capture the sunlight, though, so the bottom half of the painting was still blank. She'd done some sketches, and she knew what she was doing, so I knew it was going to be spectacular.

"Well, I do not want to interrupt the creative process, and I have a call I need to make. So, think about it. Dinner and drinks out on the town or pizza at home, either way is fine with me."

"Thanks." She gave me a kiss and went off to stare at her canvas. King Crimson fired up on the speakers. Crunchy chords, ever-changing time signatures, screechy solos. I have no idea how anyone even listens to that, but Linda can do it and paint at the same time.

I took a hike outside and dialed Amy Blackmon.

"Hello?" It was Cassie who answered.

I gulped, caught off guard. "Hi, Cassie, this is Ed Runyon. How are you?"

I instantly felt stupid and horrible. She was dying of cancer and missing her daddy. That's how she was.

"I am super!"

I almost cried. "That's good to hear. Is your mom around?"

"On the toilet. Did you find my daddy?"

"Not yet," I said. "Still trying."

"Thank you. I hope you find him. Here's Mommy."

Amy Blackmon took over. "Hello, Mr. Runyon."

"Hi. Your kid is amazing."

"Tougher than I am, for sure. Have you found something?"

"Nothing solid, but I have at least one avenue I want to check out." I was still keen on the concert angle, thinking that might lure Donny out of hiding. But my call now was to find out something else. "Ms. Blackmon, did you tell people you'd hired me?"

"Some friends at church, yes," she said. "Everyone is concerned, and I wanted to let them know what I was trying."

"That's fine, perfectly understandable. It's just that, well, I am getting death threats from somebody who really doesn't want me—or anyone else—to find your husband." I told her about the other PIs who'd been threatened.

"Nobody at our church is going to do those threats, Mr. Runyon. I guarantee that. They know I want you to find Donny before any cops do, because that's the only chance Cassie . . ."

She sobbed.

"OK, sure. I believe that. I am just trying to figure out who might know I'm on the case, that's all. Maybe one of your church friends said something to someone, I don't know. I'm grasping at straws."

"Our church is family," she said. "Sure, they'd do anything to help Donny hide, I reckon, but they love me and Cassie as much as they love him, and they know what we are up against, and they know how damned bad I want you to find Cassie's father. They would not make your job harder, Mr. Runyon. Hell, if you can narrow it down to a few square miles, these people will search for Donny inch by inch anywhere you tell them to."

"Well, then, thank you," I said.

"They're collecting money to help me pay you," she said.

"Use it for medical bills," I replied. "We'll figure the rest out. I'll keep you updated."

"Thank you, Mr. Runyon."

CHAPTER EIGHTEEN

SATURDAY MORNING, AFTER a mostly sleepless night of trying to think like Donny Blackmon but thinking about those goddamned threats instead, I made black coffee and ate a donut and sat on the deck. I am no Sherlock Holmes. You'll never catch me noticing the scuffs on a man's trousers and deducing he'd recently ridden on a fat yak at the zoo, or whatever. No. I collect facts, dump them all into a bin in my brain, and then crank a handle to mix them up. Then I pull them out randomly, like those lottery balls that decide that one guy gets seven million dollars while I wasted money on another lottery ticket.

Sometimes, that sloppy process gets me nowhere. But this time, I had an epiphany while watching rabbits dash in and out of a copse of oaks.

I poked around online, then called Detective Scott Baxter.

"Hey, Ed! What's going on?"

"Sorry to bother you on a day off."

"Day off? What the hell is that?"

I used to be a sheriff's detective. I knew Bax spoke truth. "Heard from Jerry Spence lately?"

"No, thank God. He wears on me, man."

"I'm trying to get hold of him."

"Why? He's like a chicken that won't hunt."

Chickens are not, generally speaking, birds of prey, but Baxter's metaphor machine does not use facts as operands. "He and I talked about teaming up on this Blackmon search, and I have an idea that I want to discuss with him."

"Do you have a good lead, Ed?"

"No, not really. This would be more of a side project."

Bax laughed. "I can think of smarter people you could team up with, man. Spence is not exactly smooth like toilet paper, you know? He's more of a corn cob."

I actually understood that reference. I kind of wished I didn't. "No, I think he's my guy. I am guessing you have his phone number? I checked his website, but it just has a big 'under repair' icon on it."

"Of course it does," Bax said. "Why would an independent businessman want potential customers to get hold of him? He probably owes the web host money."

"Does he have money issues?"

"Well, he sure wants that reward for finding Donny Blackmon, I can tell you that. Lights up like a pinball machine whenever the topic comes up. Give me a second, Ed. I'll get you that number."

I watched the rabbits while I waited.

"OK, here it is." He gave me the number, and I thanked him and hung up.

Spence answered promptly. "Spence Private Investigations. How can I help you?"

"You need a catchier name. Like Whiskey River Investigations."

"Runyon? Hey! What can I do for you?"

"Well, I think I brushed off that team-up idea a little too fast," I answered. "I have put a couple of things together, and, well, I'd like to talk to you. I think you can help me figure something out."

"Great! I think we can do better as a team, man!"

"Where are you now?"

"I am in Cleveland, having sausage biscuits and gravy because the lead I was chasing turned out to be a big pile of brown shit. Where are you?"

"In Mifflin County, watching rabbits. Can we meet midway, say somewhere in Medina?"

"No need for that," he said. "I am going back to Columbus today anyway, so I can just stop by."

"Well, thanks. That makes things easier for me. Do you know the town of Jodyville?"

Spence laughed. "One traffic light?"

"That's the one," I said. "They also have a bar, Tuck's Bar and Grill. Pretty good food, bad country music. Can you meet me there?"

"Sure, Ed. Gimme a couple hours."

"Great," I said. "See you then."

I walked upstairs, where Linda was in the shower. I leaned in and kissed her. "Sorry, hon, but I have to go run an errand."

"Where are you going?"

"I might beat the shit out of a guy, no big deal. Want anything from Tuck's?"

CHAPTER NINETEEN

TWO HOURS AND twenty minutes later, skinny Jerry Spence showed up at Tuck's. I saw him through the glass doors, getting out of his Toyota across the street. I told Tuck.

"You'll keep things civil, right?"

I drained my beer. "Sure. Probably." I winked.

"Don't break anything. Business has been bad. Fucking virus."

Indeed, the only people in the small bar this afternoon besides myself were Tuck and Shirley, the waitress. She was out in the kitchen, washing dishes.

"I'll be good, I promise."

I met Spence at the door. We said hello and shook hands, then I steered him toward a table under the buck's head mounted on the wall, while Willie Nelson sang "Crazy" on the jukebox. That was for my benefit, since the place was empty. As soon as a real customer came in, some sort of corporate country nonsense was going to start up, because that is what Tuck's customers want. Later tonight, after closing, Tuck would put on Led Zeppelin or something more modern, but it would involve head-banging. Lots of loud, loud head-banging.

Spence looked at the deer head and at a very large bass mounted on another wall and smiled. "Gotta love the ambiance."

"You'll like the food. I'm having a fish sandwich and a beer. How about you? I'm buying."

He nodded. "I'll let you. Just a burger for me, pickles and ketchup. And a Coke."

I went to the counter and gave Tuck the order, then added, "Give me five minutes."

He gave me my beer and Spence's soft drink, and nodded. "Yep."

While we waited for our food, we made small talk. Then Spence leaned across the table and his voice became conspiratorial. "So, what's this team-up idea, Ed? You got a line on Donny Blackmon?"

"Not so much that," I said. "But I think I have a line on another aspect of this case."

I talked vaguely, just generalities and bullshit, really, until I saw Tuck pick up his cellphone. Then I placed my glass on the table to free my hands.

Spence's phone rang, and he pulled it out of his shirt pocket. "Excuse me," he said, then he answered the call. "Jerry Spence, Spence Private Investigations."

His phone was in my hands in a flash, and I managed not to shake the table and spill my beer. I felt like a magician, producing a bouquet to the amazement of all.

Spence did not appreciate my legerdemain. "What the fuck, Ed?"

"I want to see something," I replied. "And I need your phone unlocked. So, I had someone call you. You should be happy. This way, I didn't have to beat the code out of you or hope that face recognition would still recognize you after I pounded the shit out of you."

"This is illegal," he said. He seemed very pissed.

"Yeah, sure is." I checked his iPhone. Sure enough, he had the TextNow app installed. I tapped the icon and I recognized the number that had sent me threats, although recent messages had been deleted. Spence was at least smart enough to do that.

"You've been sending me some naughty messages, Jerry."

He shook his head. "Now wait a minute, Runyon." He slid his chair back, preparing to make a break for it.

He moved faster than I expected, but my foot caught his and he went down hard. I had meant to stop him, not hurt him, but things happen and I wasn't going to fret about it too much.

Spence rolled around, bleeding from the mouth and bleating in what sounded like a foreign tongue. I think he was saying "Jesus Christ," but honestly it was more of a bellow than actual speech.

I tucked Jerry Spence's phone into my own pocket. "You've been bad, Jerry."

"You can't prove shit," he said, intelligible at last. He was holding a hand over his mouth. Some blood trickled between his fingers.

"I'm not a cop anymore, Jerry. I'm just a pissed-off private detective, and right now I don't give a shit about proving anything in court. Why did you try to chase me off of this case, Jerry? And why shouldn't I stomp your face?"

He got real quiet and wide-eyed.

I leaned forward. "Want to know how I figured it out?"

He didn't want to know, judging by his silence.

"Well, Jerry, it occurred to me to wonder who the fuck had sent me threatening messages, trying to get me off of the Blackmon case. Who the fuck would do that, I asked myself. And then it occurred to me that, maybe, someone wanted to eliminate competition for that big fat reward."

I thought that sentence deserved a little punctuation, so I grinned and tilted my head. "Want all that money for your own, Jerry?"

Tuck was watching, and standing at the center of the bar where he had a sawed-off shotgun hidden. He seemed more entertained than traumatized.

"Look," Spence said. "You got this wrong."

"I recognized the number on your app, maggot."

He removed his hand from his bloody face and smiled. It was gross. "I can explain."

"I don't give a shit. That stuff I mentioned was just speculation, of course. Not the clincher. Want to know how I figured it out? Want to know exactly where you fucked up?"

He glared at me, and sat up.

"You see, Jerry, it was that day you stopped in at the sheriff's office while I was there. You said you came in looking for Detective Baxter. It did not seem odd at the time, but I later learned you'd talked to Baxter more than once already, at the SO, and therefore you knew the records office was not where you'd find him. Right? You went to the wrong place, but you knew where the right place was. So, when that light bulb went off in my head this morning, I asked myself, why would Jerry Spence go to the wrong place on purpose? I figured maybe it was because I was in the records office. You wanted to check out the competition. How'd you find out I was on the case?"

He waved a hand at me, ignoring his bleeding chin and mouth. "Listen, Ed, I don't mean nothing by it, OK? I just need the money. Wasn't ever going to hurt anyone. Shit, I'm a pussycat."

I took a sip of beer. Jerry dragged a sleeve across his nose and made a mess of his shirt. Tuck wiped down the bar, but stayed near his gun. I hoped Tuck realized that if he fired a shotgun across the room at Spence, the spread would probably get me, too. I was pretty sure he had buckshot loaded in there. I made a mental note to go over some tactical pointers with Tuck the next time I ambushed a man in his bar.

"Seriously," Spence continued, "I should've known better, right? You're a big guy, not afraid of threats, and from what I hear you are a smart guy, too. I should've known you'd figure it out. OK. I'm sorry. You got me."

I nodded. "Hell yes, I do. What is it? Gambling? Drugs?"

"No, I'm just bad with money."

I shrugged. "Blackmail?"

His whole body froze.

I snapped my fingers. "Shit, Jerry, someone is blackmailing you?"

"No," he said. "No, not that. But . . ."

"But what?"

He tried to get up. My foot lifted and he was staring at my heel, so he gave up that notion.

"Look, Ed, I got money problems, OK? But that's none of your business."

"You made it my business when you threatened my life, remember?"

"I didn't mean it. I just wanted to chase you off the case." He stared at me and blinked. "I need the money."

"My schedule is kind of full, Jerry. I don't think I'm going to find time to care."

He stared at me, and I grew impatient. "I don't like you enough to make a day of this, Jerry."

Shirley walked out of the kitchen with a tray, stared at Spence on the floor, glanced at Tuck, then came forward and placed our food on the table. "You look good, Ed. Been OK?"

"Yeah, Shirley, thanks. Is that new ink?"

I pointed at a tattoo of a genie emerging from a lamp, on her left arm. She smiled. "Yeah, you like it?"

"It's very cool," I said. "Very 'Thousand and One Nights.'"

"It represents my wishes, you know? I like it." She pointed at Spence. "Is your friend OK?"

"He had a little balance trouble," I said. "Maybe a blood sugar issue. Food should help. Sit down and eat, Jerry. The food here is good."

Shirley nodded, and seemed to feel she was in the middle of a game show stunt. "Well, I'll get you some extra napkins for that bloody nose. You boys let me know if you need anything else." She headed back to the kitchen, double time.

I tucked into my fish sandwich. Shirley always piles on the filets when she knows it's for me.

Spence got up from the floor and sat down. He picked up the burger and took a bite. After a few moments, he said, "It's good."

"Yeah," I said. "You should have ordered fries. They're amazing."

"So, Ed, what's it going to be?"

I grinned. "Whatever do you mean, Jerry?"

"Are you going to charge me?"

I laughed. "I sure as hell ought to. But I don't think I will."

"No?"

"No. I ought to kick your ass, but I promised friends I'd try to cut down on that. But I am going to talk to a lot of other PIs and tell them what you did. I understand a few of them got threats, too. You are going to be really unpopular, Jerry, and some others might be more eager to kick your ass than I am."

"Here are the napkins, hon," Shirley said. She plopped them on the table and got away quickly. Spence started sopping up the gore on his face.

He pointed at my pocket. "Give me my phone."

"Oh," I said. "Hell no. Phones are for adults." I took a bite of crispy fish.

"That's my business, Ed, all my contacts, all my notes. I need it."

I swallowed. "Yeah, I'm sure you will feel that loss. But you're not getting it back."

"Gimme my phone!"

"You aren't mature enough to have a phone," I said. "Maybe when you are older. Your mommy and I will talk it over."

"Goddamn it, Runyon!"

"Hey, I bought you lunch," I said. "You could cut your losses and run. But if you really want the phone back, feel free to take it."

He looked me over. I am built sort of like an NFL tight end. Spence is built sort of like a lamppost.

"Goddamn it, Runyon!"

"File charges if you want, Jerry."

He got up. "Fuck you."

"I don't think you've got the stamina for that," I said.

He left.

Tuck waited until he saw Spence get in his car and pull away before he sat down. "That sniveling shit is going to be trouble, Ed."

"You think so?"

Tuck nodded. "Fuck yeah, Ed. He's big-time afraid of something, right? People who are afraid do all sorts of crazy shit. So, yeah, I'd expect trouble."

"I always expect trouble. I'll be fine."

Tuck looked at Jerry's plate. "He only ate half of the burger."

"I think he had trouble tasting it through all the blood," I said. "My fish is great, though."

Once I was back in my truck, I called all the detectives I'd talked to earlier and told them about Jerry Spence and his threats. Then I drove to the Mifflin County Sheriff's Office in Ambletown and dropped the phone into Scott Baxter's hand. "I found this at Tuck's, over in Jodyville," I said. "I think it belongs to Jerry Spence."

"The private investigator? Damn, he's a real snake in a bag, ain't he?"

"Well, he ain't no hero," I said.

Bax gave me a curious look. "Why do I think you are not telling me the whole story?"

I shrugged. "If Spence wants to talk to you about it, he can."

Bax let out a big sigh and waved the phone at me. "OK, well, thanks for turning this in. What do you think of the Blue Fury?"

I blinked. "Is that another Marvel movie?"

He shook his head. "No, Ed. Ain't you heard? Blue Fury, some shadow group in the news. They're putting up half a million for anyone who kills Donny Blackmon. Not anyone who arrests him. Not anyone who finds him. Kills him. Every paper and TV station in the state got an email from them."

I let out a deep breath, "Jesus. I never heard of them."

"Me, neither. Brand new. Happened maybe two hours ago. They say they are tired of cops being targets. They want Blackmon dead."

I was tired of cops being targets, too, but the image that filled my mind at that moment was me explaining to a dying girl that she was never going to see her daddy again because some bounty hunter got to him before I did. "Goddamn it, Bax. This is bad."

"Yeah. If Donny's going to stand trial and answer some damned questions, we'd all better hurry."

"Yeah. But it's worse than that," I said. "Anyone who even re- motely looks like Donny Blackmon might be wearing a goddamned target on his back. Can you imagine all these crazy hyped-up gun people out there thinking there's a half million out there for Don- ny's head in a wicker basket? Shit. I'll bet there isn't even a reward. Just some kooks being kooky and trying to get a guy killed. What the hell is happening to this country?"

"Don't know," he said. "Nothing is real."

Bax shrugged. I rushed out of there.

CHAPTER TWENTY

WHEN I GOT home, I gave Linda a quick kiss and headed toward the stairs.

"Hey," she said, "slow down. I've seen the news. I know why you're all tense. Are these Blue Fury people for real?"

She placed her iPad on the small table next to her recliner. I walked back to her and gave her a better kiss. "I have no idea. Never heard of them, and the radio stuff I heard on my way over here was scant at best. No one seems to know who they are. All I know is that it is really easy to set up an anonymous email account and spread whatever kind of nonsense you want."

She got up out of her recliner and hugged me. "So you think it's all fake?"

I shrugged. "I have no idea, but if somebody out there wants Donny dead, offering a half million bucks to an internet full of people who think Democrats run child sex trafficking operations out of pizza place basements would be an easy first step."

"Jesus, Ed." Linda sighed. "Things are not great, you know?"

"Not out there in the world, they're not," I replied. I held her tight. "Things are pretty good here, though."

She kissed me. "Yeah."

"I'm going to go upstairs and go online and see what I can find out. But I don't think it matters at all whether they are real or fake. It's going to cause some damned serious trouble either way, I'll bet."

She nodded. "I guess the only thing that matters is a lot of people now think they will get a bunch of cash if they kill Cassie's dad."

"Bingo. And Donny will be just as dead whether anyone actually intends to pay off that bounty or not. So, I need to go to work."

"Go," she said. "There's roast beef sandwiches in the fridge. Heat one up and take it with you."

I grabbed one, added some habanero sauce, and took it upstairs.

Once I was in my office, I popped open a beer, ate my meal, and read the news. Reporters were jumping all over the Blue Fury announcement, and the internet was full of comments. Some people loved the idea and started listing other people who needed bounties on their heads. Others wondered if this was a sign of the End Times. Reporters were either defending their editors' decisions to publicize the Blue Fury press release or arguing that they should never have amplified it at all. And all the reporters seemed to agree that once the news was out there, well, they might as well keep tweeting about it.

No one had ever heard of the Blue Fury before, but most of Twitter seemed pretty goddamned convinced the word "blue" implicated cops. A few tried to pin it on liberals in blue states.

Despite all the talking, no one provided any means for claiming the reward. There was no website or email address or phone number for Blue Fury. There was nothing, except for the possibly empty promise of a big cash prize for anyone who killed Donny Blackmon.

That prize now stood at a million dollars, according to people who did not say how they knew that.

And, of course, politicians and law enforcement all were taking this Blue Fury development very seriously, and tossing around words like "due process" and "accountable." I saw at least two senators who seemed to say those things with a figurative wink and a nudge.

Me? I took a big gulp of beer and wished I could go fishing and ignore all of it. Sometimes the world is too much.

My phone buzzed. It was Tuck.

I answered and took a wild guess. "If you are calling to tell me about the Blue Fury, I've heard."

"Damn," he said. "I thought a Luddite like you would be the last to hear."

"I'm not all over the social media like you, Tuck, but the news of the day does sometimes find me. I stopped to see Bax today, and he mentioned this new wrinkle. I've been reading about it ever since. I hope Cassie and Amy don't get wind of it. They've got enough fears already."

"This is going to complicate things for you, isn't it?"

I laughed. "Oh, hell yes. I mean, I need to find Donny before any cops do, because they might want him to resist arrest and give them an excuse. And I have to find him before any vigilantes with dollar signs floating around in their heads. And I have to find him before any other PI does, if I'm going to fulfill my marching orders from Amy Blackmon and give her husband a chance to see his girl before he goes behind bars. And . . ." I gulped. "I don't know what kind of timeline Cassie's on."

"You don't sound like you are having fun," Tuck said.

"I'm not," I replied. "I keep coming back to the fact that Donny has so far eluded everyone for months, yet was dumbass enough to leave a lot of incriminating evidence behind. I mean, the cop was chloroformed, Tuck." I filled him in on my conversation with Baxter, and then pointed out that the cops were keeping that bit of information to themselves.

"It's safe with me, man. You know that."

I did know that.

I continued. "So, chloroform implies Gullick was captured elsewhere, right? You don't gas a guy and then shoot him. You gas him to control him. So, if Donny is savvy enough to stay offline, not use a credit card, not even call his wife, why the fuck would he gas Officer Gullick elsewhere and then drag him to his own farm to kill him? Right? Who does that?"

"Nobody," Tuck said. "You're right."

I sighed. "Right now, Amy Blackmon and Cassie and I are the only three people on Earth who think Donny might be innocent. Bax, too, maybe. At least he has some doubts about Donny being the killer. Everyone else wants Donny dead."

"I believe you, too, man. Go find him."

"Yeah," I said, looking up at the sculpture Linda had made from my old guitar. "I have exactly one idea for how to do that. Thanks, Tuck. I got work to do."

CHAPTER TWENTY-ONE

I SLAMMED THE axe down sharply, but my aim was off and instead of splitting the wood, I sheared off a sliver that flew into the underbrush.

"Fuck," I said. I brushed bark bits from my forearms.

"You don't usually miss like that," Linda said.

I turned around. I had not heard her approaching. "Well, I haven't missed them all." I pointed at all the split wood lying around me and in the small trailer. It was a hot day, but if you wait until later in the year to split firewood you are likely to be doing it in the snow or rain. So, you do it when you can. And I had more than a few frustrations to take out, anyway. So, I was splitting wood.

"I could hear you cussing all the way up the hill."

"Yeah, well, the wood deserved a good chewing out."

"I brought you lemonade," she said, showing me the jug.

I leaned my long-handled axe against an oak and sat on the edge of the trailer hooked to the tractor. "Thanks. Did you put vodka in it?"

"No," she said. "You don't like vodka, and you've been in a foul mood lately, so I didn't put bourbon in it, either."

"That would be a waste of bourbon," I said.

"Yeah." She sat on the stump of a black locust we'd cut down the year before. "Are you OK, Ed? I know this case is frustrating." She handed me the jug.

I opened it and took a swig. It was tart, the way I like it. "I'm OK."

She raised her eyebrows. "You promise?"

I looked at her and saw the worry. I'd suffered from depression in the past when cases went wrong, and she and I both knew it conceivably could happen again. And she was right, I'd been a bit of a bastard the last couple of days. I could feel the tension inside me, the tingle in my arms and neck, the clenching of teeth. This hunt for Donny Blackmon was going nowhere, and it was getting to me.

But I knew a few other things, too.

I handed her the lemonade. "Thanks. That hits the spot. Look, I know this thing seems kind of sideways, but things are better now, aren't they? I'm not at the SO, so there is no boss pulling my strings. And I've got my support system around full-time now." I leaned across and kissed her. "I'm frustrated, but I'm fine. And we have a fair amount of wood ready for the fireplace."

She nodded and kissed me. "Well, then. I'll stop worrying."

"No, you won't."

We talked for a while, and Linda split some wood herself. "It's about technique, Ed. If you do it right you don't have to drive the axe like you are trying to take down the Hulk."

"I like swinging it hard," I said. Then my phone buzzed.

"Runyon," I answered.

"Detective Lannigan," the voice on the other end of the call said. "I understand you talked to Jerry Spence."

"Jesus," I said. "You guys using satellites to spy on me?"

"No," he answered, "but you know I want to find Blackmon, so I pay a lot of attention to a lot of things. I know Spence is hunting him, and I know you are hunting him, and the two of you getting together makes me think the two of you maybe think you are onto something."

I stared past the branches and into the blue sky above. "I have nothing specific."

"Look," he said. "I'm not too far from your farm. Mind if I drop by? Maybe we can brainstorm."

That sounded about as fun as felling a black locust by myself with a hand saw. But there was a chance Lannigan knew something, so I decided to give it a shot. "Give me a half hour to clean up."

"You got it."

About forty minutes later, Linda escorted Lannigan into my office. He pointed at my iPad. "Hillbilly music?"

I'd been ordering tickets for the Mud Run Bluegrass Festival, so there was a huge banjo image on my screen. "It's my jam," I told him. I decided not to tell Lannigan I hoped to find Donny there, listening to the Turkey Gravy Boys he picked with. I thought it would be a fine damned thing if I found Donny before Lannigan did. "Have a seat."

He did. "So, why did you get together with Spence?"

"To compare notes. How did you find out about that?"

"I'm a detective." Lannigan leaned forward, elbows on knees and hands clasped. He had that cop look, the one that says he knows when someone is bullshitting him. I've used that look myself, and I think I do it better, but Lannigan was no amateur. "Look, Runyon, I know a little about Spence, and I know he's a piece of shit. I just don't see a guy like you"—and he paused, and raised a hand as if to wave off some objection I hadn't made—"I know some of the local cops blame you for that thing with the football player, but hell, it was a tough call and who knows? Maybe you did right. I'm just saying you seem like a sharp guy and I don't see you working with an idiot like Spence."

I ignored his compliments. "How do you know Spence?"

Lannigan laughed. "Because he crawls up my ass all the time. Calls me, or drops by. Looking for clues in this Blackmon thing. He's so fucking desperate for that reward money, you know?"

"I know. Any clue why?"

He looked at me and shook his head. "No idea. Budget problems, I guess."

"I think that may be it, yeah," I said. "I could smell the desperation, to be honest. I asked about gambling, drugs, all that. When I asked if he was being blackmailed, he went all stiff. Like a deer in headlights."

Lannigan looked at me the way a poker player does when he is trying to decide whether to lay down his cards or fold. "I know that Spence provided Columbus PD with some intel, a decent tip from time to time, enough to make me think he probably hangs with unsavory characters. Maybe he does some unsavory shit himself. Could be someone caught him at it, and they're holding it over him for cash or dirty jobs. Makes as much sense as any theory I've heard."

I shook my head. "This is all guesswork. Did you ever get tips from Spence yourself, or have any dealings with him?"

He shrugged. "He gave me some stuff, sure, but it was minor. He took the big stuff to the guys he knew better, so I don't have facts. What I have is that I have known Spence awhile, and he was always kind of useless and squirrelly, but he was never so clingy and desperate like he seems to be now. So, yeah, maybe blackmail."

I thought for a couple of seconds. "Are you actively investigating Spence's possible blackmail situation?"

He shook his head and laughed. "Hell no. I never thought about blackmail until you brought it up, and, more importantly, I do not give three shits about Spence's problems. I want to find the guy who killed my brother officer."

"Yeah," I answered. "Nobody hired me to take care of Spence's crap, I guess."

Lannigan's stare grew cold. "But it is good to know about Spence, because this Blue Fury shit throws in a whole new wrinkle, doesn't it?"

"You mean if Spence is desperate for money he might just try to assassinate Donny instead of find him and turn him in?" I scratched my head. "A lot of people probably have that idea. Spence may be one of them."

Lannigan nodded. "A lot easier to bring in a corpse than a living man who can fight back," he said. "A lot easier. And I have to tell you, Runyon, I want to be the guy who finds that son of a bitch."

His hard eyes left no doubt on that score.

"Are you going to bring in a murder suspect or a corpse?"

"Don't much care," he said. But his expression leaned toward corpse.

CHAPTER TWENTY-TWO

THE FOLLOWING SATURDAY morning, I crawled out of my pup tent to the aroma of eggs and bacon and the high lonesome sound of someone tuning a banjo.

I stretched after having a very pleasant night's sleep. Thanks to the damned virus, I couldn't remember the last time I'd drifted off to dreamland while listening to the soft tinkle of a mandolin or the strains of a fiddle. No bands had performed yet, as the festival was officially starting today. But bluegrass crowds don't need bands on a stage to have a good time. The events draw all sorts of instrumentalists, from experts to beginners, who all know the same traditional body of work along with surprises they are willing to teach others. It's music around campfires all night, every night. Almost heaven, John Denver might have said if he were here. I wished he was.

The Mud Run Bluegrass Festival was a small affair, featuring only two days of music compared to the longer events that typically started on Thursday nights back when we all could gather and enjoy music together without masks and vaccines, but I still felt good. It felt like a step back toward normality. A baby step, but a step nonetheless.

I was still in Ohio but about three hours south of Mifflin County, surrounded by hills and trees and morning fog. Sparrows flitted about, and I could hear at least four kinds of birdsong.

I yawned, stretched again, and wished I was here just for the fun of it.

The festival was an inaugural event, on a private farm of about two hundred acres and with tickets priced to sell. The bands were not headliners, and the amenities amounted to some portable toilets and a church tent selling food. Still, there was a good crowd forming. I could see tents along the woods, and RVs beyond the concert area. The banjo picker had finished tuning and started playing "Jerusalem Ridge." A guitar had joined in, mostly strumming to keep time while the five-string played the melody.

I could not see the players. They were somewhere among the RVs. A great many of the attendees would have instruments, I knew. One of the great things about bluegrass music was the wealth of traditional songs that most all fans knew. You could find some other players, pick a song and a key and a tempo, and just let it rip. That kind of jamming was going to go on all night.

I had not brought my guitar. I don't play that well. My guitar licks had improved some during all the recent extra practice I'd gotten while staying away from people during the pandemic and not handling as many cases as I would have liked as a private investigator. But I was not yet good enough that I'd feel comfortable playing for a crowd accustomed to hearing Doc Watson or Tony Rice play. I figured if I joined in at any of the many campfire gatherings this weekend, I'd sing a bit. Not that I was great at that, either, but I'd been practicing that, too, and I can harmonize.

I had brought a different instrument, though. I had brought my handgun. I was here to work, not play.

I had come in hopes that Donny Blackmon would come out of hiding for this event. Judging by the line of trucks and campers still heading in, a lot of people had gone without live music long enough thanks to the damned virus. I hoped Donny was here.

The sun was still low, not yet risen above the trees that surrounded the field where seven bluegrass bands would take stage. The first band would not start until noon, but people already had set up lawn chairs or dropped blankets on choice spots. A stage—a flatbed trailer, really—held a small PA system, a few mics, and a young man and woman who were busy connecting cords and adjusting things.

I was camped near the woods, not far from the source of all those delicious food scents.

The orange band on my left wrist attested to the fact that my ticket to the Mud Run Bluegrass Festival had entitled me to come camp the night before, and would let me stay for shows both Saturday and Sunday. It did not cover breakfast, however, so I was going to have to fork over a few dollars to the Appalachian Christian Center if I wanted to eat. I headed toward their tent hoping to find biscuits and coffee to go with the bacon and eggs.

As I crossed the field, keeping a friendly distance from people staking their claims on prime listening spots, I kept an eye out for Donny Blackmon or any of his bandmates, the Turkey Gravy Boys. No luck so far.

Fortune smiled on me, and I was able to get myself a custom sandwich, eggs over easy with bacon and cheese stuffed between halves of a very large biscuit. The coffee was good, too. I dropped a ten into the mason jar labeled "Tips," and hoped the church would put the money to good use.

Then I began to wander. Most of the folks around me had brought cooking gear and were preparing their own breakfasts on grills set across campfires. I eventually found the banjo and guitar players I'd heard earlier. I'd decided the banjo picker wasn't Tug Burrell before seeing him; I'd heard Tug play, and he kept better tempo and picked cleaner. Still, I was enjoying the morning music. They'd moved on to "Body and Soul." Once I had them within sight, it was clear that the guitarist wasn't Blackmon. Not unless he'd managed to gain a couple hundred pounds in hiding.

No one was singing, so when I got close enough, I joined in. I couldn't wail it like Bill Monroe did, but I gave it my best and got a few nods of appreciation.

My decision to join in had two motives. One, I just love this music, and I was enjoying being around other people who loved it, too. Two, I wanted to look like I fit in. I did not want to just be some guy randomly wandering about and peering intensely into faces to find Donny Blackmon.

When the song ended, the pickers didn't even ask my name. They just smiled, and the banjo man launched into "Cripple Creek." He picked an insane tempo, but the guitar player had no trouble jumping in. I sang it, although it was uncomfortably fast and I ran some words together.

Once done, I caught my breath and the gentlemen gave their fingers a rest. "I'm Joe," the banjo player said. He pointed at his buddy. "That's Ray."

"I'm Ed," I said. We shook hands and went through the "where are you from" ritual. I lied and said I was from Akron because I did not want Donny to be roaming by and overhear anything that might bring Mifflin County to mind. I figured caution was in order.

We all went through "Blue Moon of Kentucky," this time with some awkward harmony, then I moved on. As I walked around, I kept an eye out for Blackmon, of course. But I also kept watch for Detective Jim Lannigan. I had no idea whether Lannigan was sharp enough to connect Donny's love of bluegrass music to the festival website he'd seen on my iPad, but it was within the realm of possibility. I didn't want the cop finding the fugitive first.

I even entertained the possibility that Jerry Spence might be in the crowd. The PI was about as sharp as pudding, but he was desperate for money and he'd spent a lot of time pestering people who are smarter than him, so maybe somebody had connected a few dots for him. If he was around, I wanted to know about it because he was likely to blame me for his busted face. As well he should, I guess, but my main point was that I did not want him sneaking up on me.

The crowd was growing, but none of the faces were familiar. I gazed behind the flatbed stage, where bands were offloading instruments and stepping into a rather large tent. The Turkey Gravy Boys were not yet among them, as far as I could tell.

I still had a couple of hours to go before Straight Outta Bald Creek, the first act, was supposed to take the stage. The Turkey Gravy Boys would be up afterward. I decided to change up my look, just in case anyone was on the lookout for a private detective. That seemed unlikely, but if Donny Blackmon was here, he might have friends about. I did not need one of them telling my quarry they'd seen a big guy with a Reds cap and a Bill Monroe T-shirt peering intently through the crowd. So I would change my T-shirt and skip the ballcap, and I'd look like a new man. I'd change my gait, too, and maybe slouch a bit.

When I got to the pup tent, I went straight to my truck. I opened the door, reached for my duffel bag—and froze.

The face of Tony Rice, guitarist of wide renown, stared at me from a CD cover in the console. The problem was that it should have been Waylon Jennings.

My CDs had been rearranged.

I picked up my duffel bag and closed the truck door. I was trying to look nonchalant, just in case someone was watching. I stepped to the back of the truck, tossed my cap and the T-shirt I was wearing into the bed, and pulled a fresh Cleveland Browns shirt out of the bag. Once my former shirt was in the bag, I returned it to the cab, along with my cap. I did a quick but thorough inspection, including the glove box, and noticed nothing had vanished. I did not linger over the search, though, because I did not want any watchers to realize I'd noticed the intrusion.

I made sure the T-shirt covered the Heckler and Koch VP9 clipped to my belt.

I walked toward the nearest portable outhouse, without locking the truck and without looking back. Once inside, I took care of my personal business and then peered as best as I could through the narrow slits in the plastic door. No one was near my truck or tent, nor could I see anyone paying undue attention to them.

I stepped out, washed my hands at a plastic barrel with a water pump and a bottle of soap, and resumed wandering.

Who the hell might have been in my truck? An opportunistic thief? Maybe, but the CDs were still there. I suppose a thief might have decided those weren't worth stealing in these days of music streaming. There was nothing else inside worth taking.

The glove box might have been opened, but nothing was gone.

So . . . who?

I wandered and watched and thought and basically wondered what the hell I was doing until I heard someone on the PA start welcoming everyone to the first ever Mud Run Bluegrass Festival, which prompted a chorus of whistles and wolf calls and a lot of clapping. The lawn chairs in front of the stage had multiplied prodigiously, and there was very little social distancing going on. Most of the crowd had skipped wearing masks, as had I. Vaccinations had lightened everyone's mood, we'd all gone without live music for a very long time, and damn it, it felt good to be out and about.

Also, it would be far easier for me to spot Donny Blackmon—or Spence or Lannigan, for that matter—if they weren't wearing masks. So, thank you, vaccination scientists.

I kept my distance, though. I figured the percentage of vaccine refusers in this crowd was kind of high.

The announcer apparently had stepped right out of a Grateful Dead album, complete with torn jeans, tie-dyed T-shirt, and pony-tail. "We wanna thank Mark Babcock for letting us take over his farm today! Mark, are you out there, buddy?" The announcer shaded his eyes, scanned the crowd, then pointed. "There he is! Thank Mark Babcock, ladies and gentlemen, and let's all promise not to leave a mess on his farm, hey?"

I looked in the same direction as everyone else and saw a gorilla in a cowboy hat and a black T-shirt that said "God, Guns, and Grits!" I could not tell how old Babcock was, but none of the hair sprouting between the Stetson and the T-shirt was gray. It was all brown and tangled like forest underbrush. The gorilla bowed as the crowd roared its appreciation.

"And now," the announcer said, pointing toward the five men who stood behind him, tuning instruments away from the mics, "these fellas came up all the way from North Carolina to pick for us today!" The announcer glanced back, got a nod from the banjo player as everyone stopped tuning, and finished his introduction. "Please welcome, Straight Outta Bald Creek!"

The banjo hit three grace notes and then the whole band launched into "White Freightliner Blues" at a frenzied pace. The audience hooted and hollered, and by the time the mandolin player and bass-ist fired up the harmony vocal, most of us were nodding heads or tapping feet in time. I got caught up in the moment, and for a few seconds forgot I was trying to find a homicide suspect before any-one could kill him so I could tell him his little girl was dying. Once I did remember all that, the music was less captivating.

I scanned the crowd, and I'll be damned if someone—a man, I think—didn't duck behind a tree when I looked his way.

I got over to the tree as quickly as I could, without actually running or knocking people over or otherwise tipping anyone off that I was anything other than a bluegrass lover here to enjoy the hot picking.

There was no one there, of course. And no tracks, nor telltale threads stuck to the tree bark, nor wads of tobacco nor cigarette ash nor any other goddamned thing that might have been useful to me.

I went back into the crowd, enjoying the music and looking for Donny Blackmon—and wondering if someone was looking for me.

CHAPTER TWENTY-THREE

THE TURKEY GRAVY Boys rolled up in a rusty green Ford van and parked next to the musicians' tent just as the opening act was vamping to "Molly and Tenbrooks." It's a fine song, a classic part of Bill Monroe's repertoire that relates a fictional version of an actual horse race, and the performers were trading off solos and clearly improvising a great deal. They were good at it. The Turkey Gravy Boys would have a tough act to follow, and I decided I'd have to grab a CD or two from Straight Outta Bald Creek.

A card table was being set up next to the stage, on the opposite side from the performers' tent, and boxes of CDs were made ready. By the time the opening act had finished "Orange Blossom Special," the sales table was ready, and the Turkey Gravy Boys were offstage and prepared to come up and play.

I wandered toward the sales table as the first band came down the makeshift steps. Buying a CD or two would add to my always growing collection of music by bands most people don't know, with the added bonus that it gave me a chance to get close to the stage. If Donny Blackmon was here, he was not going to miss the Turkey Gravy Boys. And if he knew these guys well, there was at least a chance he'd trust them not to shout out his name or wave if they saw him. I was hoping that was the case, and that Donny would be somewhere close to the stage.

I selected a CD, the one called *Banjos and Broadswords*, and then pretended to read the list of songs on the back as I turned around and scanned the crowd. I realized Blackmon would have drastically altered his appearance. The dark beard would be either a great deal longer or gone the way of the stegosaurus. He'd probably lost a good deal of weight, since he wasn't using credit cards and probably was low on cash. That makes Big Macs tough to afford.

But I did not see anyone who even remotely could be some version of Donny Blackmon.

I resumed meandering through the crowd while tie-dye guy introduced the band from Mifflin County. And I stayed close by—while ducking my head every time Tug Burrell or Bob Russett looked my way—as the band launched into its act. They did not fare well in comparison to Straight Outta Bald Creek, although Tug Burrell's banjo stood out.

I listened to four songs while I scanned the crowd. No Donny.

I watched the performers, too, to see if they gave any winks or nods of recognition to anyone near the stage. The only people they noticed were the young hippie girls dancing and smiling arm-in-arm under a cloud of cigarette smoke that did not smell like it came from tobacco. The girls did not notice the stares they garnered from the stage and the crowd. They were just girls, having fun.

I was not having fun at all.

The music was enjoyable enough, although it was tough to really get into it and focus on my mission at the same time. Also, I was feeling way less like a genius than I did when I bought my tickets to this show.

My mission, it seemed, was a flop.

Before long, I regretted my decision to forego a cooler full of beer. This music festival was exactly the kind of thing that should draw out a lonely man on the run. If a chance to hear his buddies playing live music for a crowd after months of everybody hiding in their homes from the goddamned COVID virus didn't bring Blackmon out of hiding, then nothing else would. I should just give Amy Blackmon my apologies and wait for some hunter to find Donny's corpse in the woods somewhere. Or watch him become some kind of D. B. Cooper legend who vanished without a fucking trace.

Either way, I wanted a drink.

The moment I realized that, I headed for the woods. I'd gone down a depressive rabbit hole a couple of times before and I had no desire to do so again. I needed to get out of sight, sit down, do some deep breathing, and stop worrying so goddamned much.

You can only do what you can do, my brain told me. *Fuck you*, my heart replied.

But another part of my brain knew what to do. I found an oak, just barely within range of the music, and pulled out my phone. I told Siri to call Hippy Angel and hoped the cellular service here was up to the task.

"Hey, Ed," Linda said. "How's it going?"

"Not good," I answered. "If Donny is here, he is laying way goddamned low."

After a brief pause, she replied, "It was still a good idea, Ed. And you told me Donny is one very careful son of a bitch, right? So don't give up too quickly. I say that, of course, as someone who is not a cop or a private detective or anything like that."

"Sure," I said, "but you're a reasonably intelligent human being, so I should listen to you."

"Hell yes, you should listen to me," she answered, and my mind's eye could see the cute scowl. "Do you want my prescription here, Ed?"

"I'm pretty sure you are going to give it to me whether I want it or not, but yeah, I want it."

I could easily envision her face, with that wry victory grin. It is one of the reasons I love her.

"OK. Well, here it is. You love this music, right? I mean, I have no idea why, all those high-pitched singers and the twang and, Jesus Christ! Why do you love it?"

I laughed. "I just do," I said.

"You just do, and that's all that matters, right? So, if Donny Blackmon doesn't show up, what's the worst thing that can happen? You get to spend a weekend listening to music you love and maybe meeting other people who love it, too, or hearing some bands you've never heard, but they end up being really awesome, right?"

"Right," I replied.

"And you wore the fucking mask, like, forever, right?"

"Yeah."

"So, you deserve a little fun, right?"

"Hell yes."

"So," she said, "enjoy your twangy music, and come home all refreshed, and think of some other brilliant way to find Donny Blackmon, OK?"

"What if I can't?"

"You will. OK?"

"OK. Linda?"

"Yeah?"

"I love you."

I could envision her smile, and I could hear it in her voice. "Yes, you do. I love you, too."

"Thanks." I ended the call.

I headed back toward the stage. Someone—I think it was Tug Burrell—was talking through the PA. "This is one I wrote myself, named for a hill where I used to drink beer and watch the stars with my buddies when we were, oh, let's just say much younger. It ain't too far from here, you know. I was born here in Pike County. Anyway, we call this 'Miller Hill' and we hope you like it."

The mandolin chopped out a muted rhythm to set the tempo, then everyone joined in. It was a hell of a closing number. No lyrics, just pyrotechnic solos against a breakneck boom-chick, boom-chick set by the bass and mandolin. They kept it going long after I emerged from the woods. The Turkey Gravy Boys clearly enjoyed performing something they created themselves.

It was the kind of music that lifts my spirits, and I was surprised to find it was working. Linda was right. I should enjoy the show and hang around tonight to see if any jammers would share a beer or two, and maybe some hot dogs or burgers, if I provided some vocal harmony. Then, refreshed, I could resume my hunt.

I checked my campsite and truck and found no sign of another visitation. I headed to the church tent and bought a hot dog with chili and mustard, plus a Mountain Dew to wash it down. I watched the Turkey Gravy Boys get into their vehicle and pull away from the musicians' tent. Donny wasn't with them.

Oh, well.

I watched the band drive away, but my heart quickened when they veered off the road and circled around the crowd. Donny's pals weren't leaving. They were headed to the campsite.

I realized I'd been a bit of a hopeful fool. Donny Blackmon had abandoned credit cards and cell phone, and had stubbornly refused to contact his wife and daughter for months. Would he show his face beneath the bright sun, where some private investigator or cop or Blue Fury bounty hunter might recognize him?

No.

But at night? At a campsite with uncertain firelight? When most people were gathered around their own fires or huddled in their tents?

Yeah. He might risk that.

CHAPTER TWENTY-FOUR

THE CAMPFIRE JAMS didn't really get going until midnight, a half hour or so after the last shave-and-a-haircut banjo riff led to a thunderous sustained chord while a guitarist soloed one more time to close out "Foggy Mountain Breakdown." Then, the crowd had roared its appreciation and started to leave the stage area. A few took their lawn chairs with them, but many just left them in place to preserve spots for the next day's show.

After the exodus, the night was filled with the sounds of instruments being tuned, with the pin-sharp plinks of the banjos and the long, sustained wails of fiddles and all the other instrument sounds fitting somewhere in between.

I had already scouted out the Turkey Gravy Boys' campsite, but I was staying away from it for now. I didn't want Cassie's dad to spot an interloper and flee. I needed to be patient.

I was wearing a blue plaid flannel shirt now over a plain white T-shirt and a straw cowboy hat that I didn't really like. The idea was to change up my appearance from earlier in the day, and I could easily alter it further by abandoning the hat or the flannel.

I still had the gun. The Blue Fury nonsense had me on edge.

I stepped up to a campfire surrounded by about a dozen college-age kids singing Bob Dylan's "You Ain't Goin' Nowhere" as two guys strummed guitars. They were following the Byrds more closely than Dylan's original, but I didn't care which version they played. I was just glad to see younger folks enjoying some good old stuff. Compared to the instrumental pyrotechnics that had been on the stage all day, the musicianship was simple, just nicely strummed chords and short picked runs between the changes. It was a good mood setter for an evening of fireside tunes.

I joined in on the next chorus, and a pretty brunette lifted a beer and smiled. She pointed at a cooler, and I helped myself to a beer. There was nothing in there that would impress Tuck, but I snapped open a can and blended with the crowd. Singing is thirsty work.

I figured I was within thirty yards of the site where the Turkey Gravy Boys had set up. I could see them moving about, silhouettes around a fire. They weren't picking yet, but I could make out the huge doghouse bass and then heard Tug tuning up his Deering banjo.

I would wait until they started playing and then let them get through a couple of songs because I guessed Donny would wait at least that long before he got too close. He'd want to make sure there were no cops watching.

The wait was pleasant, at least. The college kids were singing "Take It Easy" now, and the girls were very attractive. There are worse ways to conduct a stakeout. A couple of guys seemed a bit perturbed that I was hanging around, so I made sure not to stand too close to any of the girls. I wasn't here to fend off jealous boyfriends.

Not far away, the Turkey Gravy Boys started up "Steam-Powered Aereo Plane." I recognized Tug Burrell's touch on the five-string right away.

The brunette who'd offered me a brew earlier sidled up to me between songs and offered another. "I'm Mindy," she said.

"I'm Ed. Nice to meet you. I'll pass on the beer, though. Thanks."

"C'mon!" She laughed. "It's a party, right?"

"I had plenty before I got over here," I lied.

Mindy cracked open the can and took a healthy swig. "I'll drink it for you. Do you sing in one of these bands? You're good!"

"I played with some guys before, but then one of them hooked up with a woman named Yoko and we all started fighting and shit, and, well, it just got ugly."

"Hate it when that happens," she answered, as though the Beatles reference had gone right over her pretty little head. Kids these days. "So . . . are you camping nearby?"

"Way over that way," I answered, pointing behind me with my thumb toward a spot far from my tent. "Wife and kids are there, too. Her running sores are acting up bad, so she's in there spreading the ointment on thick. Lucky for me I only have a few." I reached up under my T-shirt and started scratching my belly.

"Oh, that sounds, um, awful," Mindy said, taking a big step back.

"It's only contagious on contact," I said.

"Of course," she replied, taking another step back. "I hope it all, um, clears up?" She looked around. "Oh, hey, look! It's Maria! Sorry, Ed, I gotta . . ."

She was already gone before she got to the word "go."

I started walking, slowly, toward Tug and his buddies. They were playing a piece I did not recognize, perhaps something they wrote themselves. The tempo was slow and lonely, featuring very loose, lazy rolls on the banjo and an almost ominous bass line while the mandolin played a sad melody atop it all. The fiddler droned a low note throughout.

By the time I was halfway to the Turkey Gravy Boys' camp, a guitar had taken over the lead from the mandolin. The player had some real chops, infusing the piece with some genuine emotion in a way the mandolinist had not.

It was dark, with clouds obscuring stars and moon, so I could see only what their campfire revealed. The players sat on lawn chairs and coolers around the fire, with two pup tents and a family-sized tent beyond them. They had just the one vehicle, the van they'd arrived in, nearby. Tents of various sizes formed a semicircle, their entrances all facing the fire. Clumsily stacked firewood threatened to topple onto a cooler. A trash bag dangled from the frame of one tent, and people occasionally strolled over to drop a beer can into it.

A small crowd, maybe a dozen people, although it was difficult to count because they were moving around, was close enough to be able to see the pickers in action. Bluegrass fans always want to see the performers' hands, in hopes of learning a few tricks.

I stopped once I was close enough to make out at least some facial features in the wavering firelight. There was bulky Tug, his eyes locked on the guitarist's fingers. There was Bob Russett, looking almost exactly like Jerry Seinfeld if the comedian played bass. He, too, seemed very into what the guitarist was doing.

The guitar player was thin in the face, and shaved bald. Tattoos all over, including his pate. He played with his head raised and moving around as though he were watching the solemn notes drift away on the night air, but his eyes were closed. Maybe he could see the music in his head.

This was a serious picker, and I hoped he would tackle something by Doc Watson next. I was lost in the music.

And then I wasn't.

The guitarist stopped. Just plain stopped. "Wait, guys."

Everyone else stopped, too.

Tug Burrell laughed. "Shit! Ha!" His head snapped back, and the red beard caught the firelight.

The guitarist opened his eyes. "I rushed that."

"Sounded good to me," Russett said.

I had not noticed any rushing. His playing had been exquisite. But I remembered Tug Burrell had told me that Donny Blackmon was a perfectionist, and how he stopped the guys mid-song if he thought he could do something better.

I looked at the guitarist's eyes, and they looked vaguely familiar, but it was too dark for certainty.

So I looked at the nose, the one I had studied in depth so I could recognize it, the one that had been broken at least once, maybe more. The one that looked kind of like a dumpling stuck to a man's face.

His weight was down at least fifty pounds from what I remembered, and the vanished beard and hair were a rather amazing transformation, but that nose was all I needed to see.

I was looking at Donny Blackmon.

"From the top," Donny said. I circled around to place myself behind him, but I kept a good distance. As far as I could tell, no one in the band had noticed me, and I wanted to keep it that way.

My heart was beating at a much faster tempo than the song they were playing.

I waited in the darkness, with Amy's letter tucked into my shirt pocket. Music from dozens of campfire jam sessions filled the air, but I focused on the song Donny and his friends were playing.

I waited until Donny took over the melody. I figured this was the moment when he was thinking about nothing but the song, or maybe not even thinking at all. Some players say they just go into a zen state, doing without thinking. Maybe Donny was like that.

I hoped he was. I hoped he'd close his eyes again, and watch the music flow through his mind. It would make my approach easier.

I had a plan. I rehearsed it in my mind a couple of times. It seemed like it might work.

Just as Donny approached the point where he'd halted the music earlier, I drew closer to the fire. I made sure to approach from an angle that reduced the risk of Tug Burrell or Bob Russett seeing me, because both would recognize my face. I didn't want them to tip Donny off.

They got to the tough guitar lick, one that required Donny to bend two strings at once, and I half expected him to halt the music again. But he nailed it this time, and smiled big while his band mates nodded their respect. The song went on, and I waited to make my move.

They ended the piece with a very nice fade-out. They all were smiling by the last lonely chord. It was clear that Donny's guitar elevated the whole band.

I stepped up to Donny, with my back to Burrell and Russett. "Man, that was stellar picking. You have real talent."

I got no further.

Donny sprang up like a spooked cat, and the guitar came flying at my head. I managed to duck, but Donny was running before the guitar landed on the grass with a discordant sound behind me.

The crowd produced a chorus of confused sounds. Incoherent exclamations of surprise were peppered with the usual phrases.

"What the fuck?"

"Holyyyyy . . ."

"Jesus!"

"Look out!"

Donny was fast, I'll give him that. A price on your head lends wings, I guess. He took off like a rocket, and curled around the crowd, using them as unsuspecting blockers and increasing his chances of getting out of my sight.

"Damn it," I muttered. I took off after him as hard as I could go. If he managed a decent NFL wide receiver move and vanished into the darkness, I might never get another chance.

It isn't easy to yell at a full run, but I gave it my best. "Donny!" I got maybe a dozen long strides before someone grasped my ankle and a gunshot rang out through the night.

I did a face-plant, and heard the college girls cry out in high-pitched squeals. Their guys were yelling out more variations on the themes of "holy shit" and "what the fuck." Musicians at the other campsites kept picking, of course. To them, it might have been a firecracker, or just someone showing off a new gun to a buddy. This was rural Ohio, after all.

"What's happening?" That plaintive wail may have been Mindy, but who really knows.

I was in no position to explain what was going on, though, because I was getting kicked in the head and ribs, and somebody had planted a foot on my back.

I reached out wildly and grabbed a handful of something that felt like denim. I rolled and pulled as hard as I could, and heard at least two people topple. That felt good.

I reached for my gun. It was not there.

I tried to get my feet under me, thinking to just bull my way out of this mess. It was a futile maneuver, though, as the kicks kept coming. I curled up like a lineman clinging to a fumbled football. I tried to explain how I was just a nice private investigator from Mifflin County, here to simply deliver a message to Donny Blackmon from his wife and his dying child, but it came out mostly like grunts and sudden inhalations, and I don't think my attackers were in a listening mood, anyway.

In the distance, another shot rang out.

What the fuck was going on?

I tried to roll. I tried to gain my feet. I got to my knees, and then someone shoved a cloth into my mouth and threw some sort of fabric over my head. Suddenly, I decided to put all of my effort into just breathing.

I never passed out, but I was soon beyond fighting. The kicks and punches never stopped until my ankles and wrists were bound in what I supposed were zip ties. I'd had those used on me in training, once.

My wrists were behind me, of course, because that is just how my luck runs.

My phone buzzed in my shirt pocket. Someone grabbed it.

Then I was hoisted off of the ground and carried. I heard a zipper, like a tent being opened up, and then I was tossed inside onto something that felt like a cot.

Next, I smelled rank tobacco and heard a quiet voice close to my head. "You cry out, you say one goddamned thing, and I will fucking blow your head clean off."

The next sound I heard was a magazine being shoved into a handgun.

CHAPTER TWENTY-FIVE

I HEARD THE tent entrance zipper being pulled, and tried to control my breath, which wasn't easy because I had a mouth full of bandana or something and my head was wrapped in some kind of fucking bag or cloth or whatever. I spent at least a couple of minutes wondering if I was going to suffocate before I convinced myself that I truly could breathe, if I remembered to remain calm.

Once that very important issue was settled, I had other questions.

Who did the shooting? Was it a bounty hunter who figured out what was up, or was it one of Donny's buddies trying to kill me?

What the fuck had just happened?

I did a mental inventory of my body. I've been in a few scrapes, and I could tell I was going to have some serious bruises. But nothing was broken, and I did not feel any of the telltale signs of blood loss—dizziness, irregular heartbeat, chills. I would hurt, but I could still function.

I wriggled around a bit on the cot, trying to assess just how screwed I really was. The results were not reassuring. The zip ties bit into my wrists, and they were bound tightly. My ankles were well wrapped, too. I could abandon any dreams of getting to my feet and running for my life.

I couldn't see a damned thing, either.

At least I could hear. I could just make out voices if I concentrated.

They were not happy voices. They were intense growls, probably through clenched teeth and involving some occasional flying spit.

"Fucking bounty hunter, I say."

"Or a fucking cop," someone else answered.

A couple more voices chimed in. All were fueled by anger, suspicion, or confusion. They were trying to keep their voices low, but they were failing.

"I say we kill him," one voice said. That shut the other guys up, leaving me with nothing to hear but the distant sounds of bluegrass and folk music and my own heart beating. I'm pretty sure my heart was playing at the fastest tempo.

"That is goddamned stupid," someone finally replied. "What the fuck are we going to do with the body, huh?"

"Guys, it ain't right to kill him," a far more reasonable gentleman opined. He instantly became my favorite, and I nicknamed him Solomon.

"He's a goddamned bounty hunter, man! Live by the sword, die by the sword, right?" In my mind, I labeled this guy as Mr. Vicious. "You go hunting dangerous felons for a living, man, that's dangerous work. Bet those bastards die all the time." I could tell he said "dangerous felons" with air quotes. His sarcasm was almost at Bill Murray's level.

"Fuck yeah," someone answered Mr. Vicious. I wasn't sure if I'd heard this guy speak yet, but his accent was from at least two states farther south than any I'd heard so far, so I thought of him as Tennessee.

"We are on a farm in the middle of goddamned nowhere," came the reply from Mr. Vicious, and it had a bit of a jaunty tone, kind of like the one I'd always imagined Jack the Ripper used when reading aloud his demented little notes to London's Metropolitan Police Service. There was an air of "no one will ever be able to figure this out" in that voice.

"We can do whatever we like," the man added. "We can drag him off into the woods, slit his fucking throat, wait for him to bleed out, and then dig him a shallow grave."

Another voice, thankfully sounding kind of skeptical, replied, "What if someone knows he came here? What if the cops come looking for him?"

The jaunty voice had an answer, of course. "It's a big fucking farm, ain't it? What are they going to do, dig it all up? And how many fucking people are here, anyway? A few hundred? Even if they find his corpse, how are they going to pin it on us? Right?"

"We can't kill him," Solomon said in a stage whisper. "It ain't right. I can't even believe we are seriously talking about this."

I really, really wanted to jump into the conversation at this point and add a couple of amens. But when I tried, my muffled voice just sounded like someone in a horror movie, trying to shout from a coffin buried under six feet of dirt.

My captors heard it, though. I heard the tent unzip, and I felt something that probably was the business end of a handgun against my head. I wondered if it was my own H&K.

"One more time, motherfucker," a voice whispered. "I got a silencer, you know? I could pull the trigger right fucking now, and no one would hear anything except maybe you and me might hear a little piffle or something. And you might hear your own head being torn up inside for an itty bit. So, if I was you, I'd shut the fuck up."

I tried to nod. I had no idea if my antagonist would even realize I was nodding, since I had no fucking idea what my head was encased in. But I nodded. Oh, hell yes, I nodded.

"Good boy," the menacing voice said. I heard him walk away, followed by the tent zipper.

I want it on the record that I did not piss my pants at this point. Don't ask me how.

A few seconds later the voices resumed. Mr. Vicious wanted to shoot me in the head right now and just burn the cot, the tent, and anything else that got my blood on it. He wanted a real bonfire. He even suggested throwing my remains on it.

"It won't all burn up, I don't think," one skeptic said. "The bones, I mean. I think you need a really hot fire for that, like an oven or something."

One guy suggested dragging me into the woods and leaving me tied to a tree. Someone wondered if that might result in me starving to death or being eaten by coyotes. One person, perhaps more experienced in the ways of crime than the others, pointed out the risk of me surviving long enough to be found, and then possibly being able to help the cops find the guys who captured me. At least two dudes said they didn't fucking care.

I, of course, cared very much.

Solomon piped up. "Damn it, fellas, there's police who will know what to do with this guy. We should just turn him in. So far, we ain't done nothing more wrong than a citizen's arrest, right? This guy was armed, confronted us, fought with us, we subdued him out of self-defense, right?"

"Police is the ones that want to kill Donny," Mr. Vicious answered, followed by a chorus of "hell yeah." Another guy added some sterling logic. "If we bring cops into this, they're just going to ask us about Donny. Don't want them figuring out he was here, do we?"

More amens.

"Think they heard the shots?"

That drew laughter. "Everybody heard the shots," Mr. Vicious said. "But it's a summer Saturday night in Pike County, Ohio, man. Everybody in this county has heard a shot or two sometime tonight, right?"

"Which of you fuckers fired?"

No one answered that. They just chuckled. I heard the pop of a beer can tab.

These guys sounded like they would go on all night. I started focusing on how I could get myself out of this mess.

These guys were Donny's friends, so priority one, in my mind, was convincing these guys I was not here to arrest or kill Donny Blackmon. I figured the only way I could do that was by employing my amazing rhetorical skills, so I needed to get the goddamned cloth out of my mouth and off my face.

Of course, I had no idea how to do that.

I tried to calm myself and assess the situation. I was bound with zip ties and gagged, and lying on a cot.

Cots have frames. Frames imply metal, wood, or plastic.

Frames are solid parts, something fabric or zip ties can be rubbed against until they give. It might take a million years, but in theory, it should work.

Good boy, Ed. You are doing great.

The voices outside the tent kept talking, but I was no longer focused on what they said. I was straining my neck, trying to find the frame of this fucking cot so I could free my head from whatever the fuck was surrounding it.

And yes, I was fully aware I needed to pull this miracle off before the committee outside formed a consensus and decided on exactly the most efficient and expeditious way to kill me. Solomon was outnumbered, and I was a big damned inconvenience. Can't just leave potential witnesses lying around. It simply isn't done, old sport.

After approximately two hundred attempts, give or take a million, I finally managed to get the fabric that was covering my head caught against the end of the cot frame and wiggle my head free. I was surprised I hadn't broken the cot with all my gyrations.

I did manage to scrape my cheek, of course. I couldn't tell if I'd drawn blood, but it felt deep enough.

The covering, whatever the hell it was, fell to the tent floor. I inhaled deeply through my nose and congratulated myself on my amazing success.

Outside, I heard one guy whisper that he had a big jug of gasoline in the van and maybe that could make a fire hot enough to burn my corpse to ash.

I tried to look around me. It was still dark outside, but the campfire was bright enough to throw some light through the tent fabric. I was in a family-sized tent, on one of two bunks within it. Duffel bags and blankets were on the floor around me. The men discussing whether to let me live or die were shadows on the tent wall.

My mouth was full of foul-tasting cloth. I craned my neck again and tried to get the fabric hooked on the edge of the cot frame.

The most militant of the voices outside suggested four more ways I could be killed, one of which involved drowning in a creek, before I got the goddamned thing out of my mouth. It was a bandana, probably full of sweat and hair, possibly full of lice.

Instead of puking, I inhaled sharply. That hurt, because my throat was raw.

Then, I shouted. I was hoarse after being gagged, naturally, but I managed to get it out.

"I'm not a cop! I'm not a bounty hunter! Amy Blackmon hired me to get a message to Donny!"

Well, by God, that shut my captors up.

CHAPTER TWENTY-SIX

SOMEONE RIPPED OPEN the tent zipper and aimed a supernova at my face.

"Is that you, Runyon?"

It was Solomon, aka Tug Burrell, the banjo man. I recognized the voice now that my ears were uncovered. I had already pushed my ability to speak coherently to its current limitation, so my prayer of thanks was all in my head, but it was no less heartfelt.

"You know this son of a bitch, Tug?" That was Mr. Vicious, standing behind the banjo man. The rest of the gang were still behind them, fighting for a glimpse of the man they thought they might kill and burn.

"Don't know him," Burrell said. "Met him once. He came around asking questions about Donny, said Amy hired him."

I got my lungs working properly again, and talked with difficulty. "Yes. Ed Runyon. Private investigator, messenger boy, bluegrass fan, and sometimes captive." I still couldn't see. "Could you aim the flashlight elsewhere?"

He did.

"And can I have some water? That thing you shoved down my throat tasted like sweat and bugs."

"Get a bottle of water in here," Tug said.

"Ain't no damned water," someone answered from outside.

Tug sighed. "The other cooler. One for beer, one for pop and water, remember?"

"I only knew the beer one. Hold on."

The water showed up quickly after that. Tug held it for me, and I drained the bottle instantly. It was icy cold, and it felt really good.

Vicious crowded his way past Burrell and pointed a pistol at my face. "He could be lying," he said. "There's a lot of money on Donny's head."

I shook my head slowly. "I'm not after that. You can call Amy Blackmon and ask her." I thought about the note she'd written, which I hoped was still in my pocket. I decided against mentioning it, though. She'd intended it for Donny alone.

Burrell spat at the ground. "I did call her," he said. "After you came to my place. She said she hired you, wouldn't say why."

"She's a proud woman," I said. "She's got her reasons, I guess. But all I am supposed to do is find Donny and tell him what she wants me to tell him."

"And what is that?" Mr. Vicious said, sounding a little like Dirty Harry but looking more like Jerry Seinfeld. Now that my eyes were almost working again, I recognized the bass player, Bob Russett. He who hates cops.

I was no longer a cop, of course, but I doubted that sort of nuanced thinking would impress Russett, so I didn't mention it. "Look," I said, "she hired me to tell Donny something, not to tell everyone else. If she wanted the world to know, well, there's an internet—she could use that and make a big announcement. But she didn't. She hired me. So let me go or shoot me, but don't expect me to spill Amy's secrets."

"Fuck you, asshole." The gun went against my head.

"Bob, calm the hell down." Tug Burrell stepped up and lifted Russett's gun arm, and Russett relented. He looked disappointed, though. I think Bob was really, really hoping he'd get to kill someone. He'd sounded rather enthusiastic about drowning me. He'd said it might be a way to make my death look like an accident. "Pour whiskey all over his shirt, unzip his fly—hell, it'll look like he fell into the water and *drownded* while he was taking a piss!"

I was hoping I'd get a chance to riff on his pronunciation of "drownded," but at the moment that was a secondary concern.

Tug reached down to his boot and came back with a Bowie knife. He looked rather like a menacing Santa Claus, with a white beard saturated with blood. I wondered if he'd just decided letting his buddy shoot me would be too loud.

"Roll over," he said. "I'll cut the ties."

I followed orders, and in a few seconds I was sitting up and rubbing my raw wrists. "Thanks," I said.

He leaned close and looked at my face. "We roughed you up pretty good. You going to be OK?"

I actually laughed. "Well, it definitely was more painful than the last time I got captured, but I'll live."

"You get captured a lot?"

"Last time, it was by a college chess club."

He looked at me for a while, trying to decide whether I was putting him on. I wasn't.

"Huh," he finally replied.

I shrugged, moved my legs a bit, and stretched my arms. Everything hurt. But I did not have time to worry about that. It was my turn to ask questions, and I had a great one.

"Are you able to get in touch with Donny?"

"Huh?"

"If you are, my mission is almost over. I'm not trying to bring him in or hunt him down. Seriously. I just want to give him Amy's message. If you can get it to him, I'll write it down and seal it in an envelope. You just give it to him, and he'll do whatever he needs to do." I wasn't about to hand over Amy's letter, because I had no idea what was in it. But I could craft one of my own and give them that.

"You don't think I'll read it?"

I looked him in the eyes. "No, I don't. Russett, he'd read it, for sure. By the way, Bob, it's 'drowned,' not 'drownded.' Jesus, man, if you're going to kill a guy, at least learn how to say it right."

"Fuck you," Russett said.

I turned my attention back to Tug. "These other guys? They'd probably read it, too. But I trust you. If you tell me you'll deliver it unread, I'll believe you."

"Why?"

"Because you thought killing me was the wrong thing to do."

He nodded. "You're OK, Runyon. I think you're OK. But we can't get hold of Donny."

"You wouldn't kid me, would you?"

Tug shook his head slowly. "I wish I could contact him. I truly do. But we only prayed he might show up here today. Had no idea if he would or not. Glad he did, but now that somebody came this close to nabbing him . . ."

"I wasn't here to nab him."

Tug laughed. "Hell, I know that and you know that, but Donny don't. I never seen him move that fast. All that weight he lost, I guess. But he'll learn from his mistake. Ain't no way he'll get anywhere near us now. You, me, the world, we ain't gonna see him again."

I sighed. "You're probably right. Can I have my gun back, please?"

Tug looked around. "Which one of you boys has Mr. Runyon's gun?"

"It's a real nice gun," someone outside the tent said.

Tug sighed. "Are we thieves?"

It took a while for him to get an answer. "No."

"Then let's give it back to him. I don't think he'll shoot us."

The gun was passed forward. "I'll need my phone, too, please."

"I got that," Tug said. "Here you go."

CHAPTER TWENTY-SEVEN

DAWN WAS TEASING the sky just beyond the distant tree-topped hill by the time I got back to my campsite. There were more bands scheduled to play on Sunday, but losing my best shot at finding Donny Blackmon and being pummeled by the Turkey Gravy Boys had momentarily spoiled my appetite for bluegrass.

I was also disheartened by my futile attempt to find Donny's trail in the dewy morning grass by the light from my phone. I had found the spot where I was gang-tackled. The ground was pretty chewed up there. But the rest of it had been trampled by music lovers and drunks looking for a dark place to piss to avoid the long hike to the portable toilets. I'm not a bloodhound or a Tolkien ranger, either, so there was no way I was going to find my quarry that way.

I checked the truck and interior of the tent for signs of another visitor. All seemed well.

I headed for the urinal station first and used the barrel-and-faucet contraption to clean up a bit, then returned to my camp and changed into cleaner clothes. After packing away the tent and everything else, I got into the Ford, popped in a Willie Nelson disc, and drove to Waverly, a town of about four thousand or so and the Pike County seat.

My mood was too low for Willie to pick me up. I needed a new plan, else I was going to have to go tell Amy Blackmon I'd failed. Worse, I was going to have to tell little Cassie.

How the hell was I going to be able to do that?

Just as Willie and the band started playing the raucous live version of "Whiskey River," the song for which I'd named my PI business and one that usually lifts my spirits, I spotted Diner 23. It was just off the main highway and modeled after an old-fashioned rail car. Sometimes places like that have great breakfasts and good coffee, and I needed both. I had a lot of thinking to do.

The parking lot was mostly full, which boded well for the prospects of good food, but I managed to squeeze the F-150 into a spot not too far away. I jumped back into the truck almost as soon as my second foot hit the ground, though.

A familiar face had stepped out of the diner.

Jim Lannigan, the Ambletown cop who wouldn't take his wife's calls and who seemed just a bit too eager to find Donny Blackmon for my tastes.

There could be only one reason for Lannigan to be in Pike County, Ohio, of course. He'd come looking for Donny. But how had he picked up the trail?

I had not yet alerted anyone that I'd had Donny within reach just hours ago. I wanted to give myself a chance to find him before any cops or bounty hunters did, and I was keenly aware that some of the former could be among the latter. As soon as word got out that Blackmon had been sighted, the area would be thick with both. And if reporters picked up on that, so would anyone who dreamed of becoming an instant millionaire by fulfilling the Blue Fury bounty.

No, I was going to keep my cards close to my vest. Such as they were.

So how had Lannigan sussed it out? Had he followed me down here? Had he hidden a GPS tracker on my truck? I've had that happen before, and trust me, it sucks.

Or had Lannigan gleaned more than he'd let on from his brief glimpse of my iPad screen that day he'd visited my office? Maybe he'd asked himself if I was buying tickets just for the music, or if maybe I had a line on Donny Blackmon. Hell, I suppose it was possible Lannigan had just figured it all out on his own, with no inspiration from little ol' me.

However he figured it out, he was here. That was for damned sure.

But he wasn't at the Mud Run Bluegrass Festival.

He was at a diner. And that, of course, got all kinds of wheels and cogs churning in my brain.

As I watched him walk toward his dark SUV, I called the Ambletown Police Department. I used the non-emergency line, because I'm not a dick.

"Ambletown Police," the young man on the other end answered.

"Hello," I said. "My name is Ed Runyon. I'm a private investigator."

"Yes, sir," he replied. I could tell by his tone that he recognized the name. My actions in the hunt for local football hero Jeff Cotton probably still inspired conversations and much swearing among Mifflin County peace officers. This young man handled things professionally, though. "What can I do for you, Mr. Runyon?"

"I was hoping to drop by there and talk to Detective Lannigan. Is he in today?"

"He is not on station at the moment," the man said. "I can take a message and relay it to him, and he can contact you himself."

"That's OK," I said. "I think I have his number, come to think of it. I'll try that. Thanks for your help."

"Have a good day, sir."

I hadn't really expected the dispatcher to tell me that Lannigan had called in sick, or taken a personal day, or left his jurisdiction to look for the suspect in Brandon Gullick's homicide. Dispatchers are stingy with such information, as well they should be. But sometimes you get lucky and someone blurts something out, or they ask someone nearby if Lannigan's in, and you pick up some information in the background. No such luck this time.

I could not help but wonder why Lannigan was not at the bluegrass event if he thought that's where he could find Donny.

When Lannigan rolled out of the diner's parking lot, I followed him, my grumbling stomach be damned.

CHAPTER TWENTY-EIGHT

I FOLLOWED LANNIGAN a short distance south on U.S. 23 to the Ameristay Inn and Suites, across from a Rooster's restaurant. He parked very close to the front entrance. I parked at a distance, with a few intervening cars and trucks between my vehicle and his because I did not want the cop to recognize my truck.

I grabbed my binoculars from behind the seat and watched him walk in. I had a better view than I'd had before, and I noticed some details. He was wearing jeans with grass stains at the knees. His flannel shirt was tucked in nicely, but there was a significant tear on the upper left sleeve. And he had scratches on his face.

He sure as hell did not look as though he'd slept in a hotel, and I doubted his wife had let him leave the house in the wee hours looking this way, no matter how much they didn't talk to one another. It seemed unlikely that he'd gotten up early and driven three hours or so this morning just to grab a diner breakfast and find a hotel room.

He'd been up to something else last night, and I had a pretty good idea what.

If I was right, Lannigan most likely would grab a shower and get a few hours sleep. I needed to do the same.

After a few minutes, the cop exited the hotel and grabbed a duffel bag from his vehicle, then went back inside.

A rather wild hypothesis was forming in my head, and I decided to start testing it. I pulled out of the lot, then called the detective himself.

He didn't answer with a hello. "Runyon?"

"Yeah, hi. Listen, I hope I didn't wake you up or anything. I know it's early, but I wanted to let you know. I came within a frog's hair of catching Donny Blackmon last night."

He paused a little longer than seemed natural. "He got away?"

"Yeah, I was tackled by some of his friends and he—"

"Jesus, Runyon, where are you? Are you OK?"

"Yeah, just roughed up a bit."

"Where did you see Blackmon?"

"He's in Ohio, Pike County. Although, he may be somewhere else by now. Took me a while to get back into contact with the world."

"Where are these friends? I want to interrogate them."

"No idea," I said. "They dropped me, kicked me, beat me, and then scattered."

"I need names."

"Sure. I'll text them to you. The ones I have, anyway. Didn't get them all."

"Jesus," he said. "Where the fuck did you say you are?"

"I am in Waverly, a few hours down south from Mifflin County. There is a bluegrass festival here, and I thought it was the kind of thing that might bring Donny out of hiding."

"Yeah?" I could almost hear the wheels turning in his head. "Are you staying there?"

"Of course," I answered. "I figure Donny is running again, but he probably hasn't gotten far, and maybe he's been down here for a while, right? So I'm going to poke around, ask questions, see if I can draw a line on him."

"Good, good," he said. "Did you get a good look? Have you got an updated description?"

"Sure," I said. "It was by firelight, but I got a decent look." I told him what I'd seen.

"OK, have you given this to the police yet?"

"I called you first. I know this case is important to you."

"Yeah," he said. "I appreciate that. Officer Gullick was one of ours. I want Ambletown PD to bring his killer in. And by that, I mean I want to bring him in myself. Look, I think I can take the day off. How long is the drive down there?"

"About three hours," I said.

"You at a hotel?"

"No. I camped at the festival. I broke camp, though, because there is no chance in hell Donny will go back there. I practically had him by the collar, Jim."

"OK, well, you tried. And you did good to call me. I appreciate that. I'll get out the word. What's the town there, again? Waverly?"

"That's where I am now, yeah."

"Fine. They got a McDonald's?"

"Everyone has a McDonald's."

"Meet me there at noon. I'll hit the road as soon as I can."

"See ya there," I said. "With any luck, I'll have more to tell you when you get here."

"Hope so. Bye."

I hit the McDonald's for a sausage muffin but ordered orange juice instead of coffee. Then I drove north, found a big parking lot outside a Kroger grocery, and set an alarm to wake me before noon. I settled down in the truck for a nap.

As I tried to drift off to sleep, a memory seeped up from some-where in my brain. I once heard crows somewhere close by on a foggy December afternoon. Despite the screams and caws, I could not see them. I kept looking, and eventually the birds emerged from the mist. Not all of them, though. They were circling, drawing near enough for me to make them out in the mist, then circling away to fade once more into nothingness. I could hear dozens, but never saw more than five or six at a time.

I'd watched that sky dance for probably ten minutes and started to understand why some people believe in ghosts. I was watching ghost crows.

A similar thing was going on in my mind now. I wondered why Jim Lannigan had lied to me. Potential reasons took shape, circled away, and disappeared. By the time I drifted into sleep, I'd started wondering if maybe Detective Jim Lannigan needed a whole lot of money, and if he thought killing Donny Blackmon might get him some.

CHAPTER TWENTY-NINE

THE FIRST THING I did when I woke up was to call Mifflin County Sheriff's Detective Scott Baxter.

"Hello, Ed," he said. "How are you this fine day?" Baxter always managed to sound like he was glad to hear from anyone who called him. His house could be in flames, and I bet he'd still pick up the phone with a cheerful "Hello, Ed."

"I'm OK, Bax. I was just calling to see if there had been any new developments in the Donny Blackmon hunt."

"Sorry, Ed, but no. Every trail's gone cold as frog spit."

I had no idea what that meant. Bax probably had no idea, either. "Nothing at all, huh? Damn. I was hoping there had been some kind of sighting or breakthrough or something. Anything on the murder of Officer Gullick?"

"I suspect we'll find out more on that second one once we find the answer to the first," Baxter replied. "Ain't no sign that anyone else but Donny killed Officer Gullick, if that's what you're asking."

"Well, thanks anyway, Bax. Have you talked with Lannigan lately?"

"No. Should I? Are you chasing down something yourself, Ed?"

"Trying to, but not really getting anywhere."

"Uh, OK." He sounded kind of skeptical.

"What is it, Bax?"

"Well," he said, and I could almost hear the gears in his mind whirring, "it's kind of odd, you calling out of the blue for an update. On a Sunday. And, well, when I said there was nothing new on Donny, you sounded almost like I'd told you something you expected to hear, not surprised at all."

Scott Baxter was maybe a better detective than I'd given him credit for, and I wondered if I could shake him off the trail. "You heard something in my voice, is that what you are saying?"

"Indeed, Ed. I've known you awhile, and worked with you. You are trying to confirm something, or figure something out. You're like an old dog with a new bone, can't let stuff go, and you gotta keep gnawing. But you don't just randomly call for updates. What the hell is going on?"

Now it was my own head buzzing with spinning gears. If I told Bax what I knew and what I suspected, Pike County would soon be swarming with cops. I'd miss my chance to fulfill my promise to Amy Blackmon and Cassie, and worse, might get Donny Blackmon killed in the process.

If I kept my information and suspicions to myself, however, I was withholding evidence in a murder investigation. It was not a comfortable dance, I admit.

I made up my mind more quickly than I thought I would. "Bax, it is true. I think I might have an angle on all this, and I wanted to check out what you'd heard. But I am mostly guessing right now, you know? I don't have anything concrete. Give me some time to confirm some shit, and if it turns into anything worth our time, you'll be the first person I call."

"I have a whole sheriff's office here bigger than a family farm, Ed, damn it, so if you need something checked you tell me and I'll get the chickens to scratching right here. We'll check it out faster than you can on your own, I'll promise you that."

"Probably," I answered. "It's a real slim thread, though, Bax. And I don't want to waste your time."

"Hunting down the killer of a brother peace officer is never a waste of time." I could tell I was making Detective Baxter angry. I'd never really seen that before. "Where are you?"

"Out of town," I said. "Look, if my hunch pays off, I'll get right back to you. Deal?"

"Ed, this is serious stuff."

"I know. I'll call you soon, either way, and fill you in."

I ended the call. So Ambletown Detective Jim Lannigan, he who was so determined to be the one to find murder suspect Donny Blackmon, had not bothered to report to other law enforcement agencies that Blackmon may have been spotted in Pike County the previous night. That, you could say, made me even more curious. I started gnawing on that bone.

Lannigan had told me he was fairly new to Ambletown PD, having previously worked as a detective in Columbus. I knew a detective in Columbus, so I called her.

Shelly Beckworth did not answer, but I got her voicemail. "Shelly, I need a favor. Do you know a cop named Jim Lannigan, used to work as a detective in Columbus? Now he's in Ambletown, and I need to know more about him. Especially I want to know if he has any big debts, gambling issues, money worries, anything like that. Give me a call when you can. Thanks."

I remembered the man ignoring his wife's calls and wondered if he was expecting to get soaked in an upcoming divorce. That could make a man desperate for new income. Maybe the bounty promises from Blue Fury were looking pretty good to Lannigan.

I rolled into the McDonald's lot and waved at a pair of sheriff's deputies who were standing next to their patrol vehicles and laughing about something. They weren't on a high alert any more than Bax had been.

I spotted Lannigan's vehicle farther back in the lot, but he wasn't in it.

I walked inside and wondered if Lannigan was going to lie to me some more.

CHAPTER THIRTY

I ORDERED A Big Mac and coffee, walked past a family of five and a couple of guys in MAGA hats, and sat down with Lannigan.

"You look like hell," he said.

"Camping will do that to you. So will getting beat up. Did you get roughed up, too?"

He'd cleaned up and changed clothes, but he had a Band-Aid on his right cheek. The cop looked like he could use about nine more days of sleep, too.

"Got in a hurry to get down here, cut myself shaving," he replied.

I pretended to accept that answer. "Did you have an easy drive down?"

"Yeah, you just stay on the highway, right? Get to it. When did you see Blackmon, and where?"

"I told you, at the Mud Run Bluegrass Festival, not too far from here on some guy's farm. Late last night, among the campers."

He shook his head. "All that hillbilly music," he said. "Norman Blake and shit. And why aren't you out there asking questions?"

"Because I was out there all day yesterday and never saw him until after midnight. It's a good-sized crowd, but not so large that I wouldn't have seen him if he was there. No, he stayed hid and did not come out until after dark. He is a very careful son of a gun, re-member. So, I doubt seriously anyone there saw him, except his bud-dies, and they scattered after tackling me."

Lannigan almost snarled. "You better believe I'll be asking them questions. But you should've asked around. Low odds that anyone saw Donny, maybe, but it's standard procedure. You ask questions, even if you think you already know the answers."

"I'm not a cop anymore, right? So, screw procedure."

Lannigan was turning out to be a pretty good poker player. Lec-turing me about procedure had been a masterful touch. My buddy Tuck tells me my poker game suffers from the same problem as my chess game. Lack of patience.

"So, Jim, why the fuck isn't Pike County crawling with cops right now?"

He became very alert. "Excuse me?"

"I told you this morning that I'd spotted Public Enemy Number One last night and almost grabbed him. But here it is half the day gone and you're the only cop who's shown up to do anything about it. Where's the command post? Where's the SWAT van? Why aren't you out there talking to those happy deputies in the parking lot? Where's the public information officer to tell the gathered members of the press that we can't confirm anything for now but we'll let you know at the appropriate time?"

Lannigan leaned forward. "What are you implying, Runyon?"

I glanced outside. The chatting deputies were gone.

"Just wondering why a stickler for procedure such as yourself wouldn't have let other cops know what I'd told you," I said. "Why are you keeping such secrets, Jim?"

"I told you, Ed. I liked Gullick. He was a brother officer. I want to be the one to bring his killer in."

"Dead or alive."

"Alive, if I can," he said, his eyes glaring at me. "But the other way is fine, too."

"The other way pays better, doesn't it?"

I thought he might come out of his chair and throttle me. "What are you saying, Runyon?"

"I'm saying maybe you'd like to rake in some of that Blue Fury reward money for killing Donny Blackmon." I leaned across the table, too. "You can't do that if someone else gets him first, can you? Hence, your silence regarding Donny's whereabouts."

Lannigan actually laughed. "Heh, well, you don't know me, I guess. So, I'm going to let that slide. Maybe." His eyes did not match his words, though. His eyes were looking around the eatery, glancing through the big plate-glass windows and blinking away beads of sudden sweat.

I clearly was missing something, and I stared at him for thirty seconds trying to figure out what it was. By the end of that half-minute, we were no longer playing poker. We were playing chicken.

"I have a gun aimed at your belly right now," he said quietly. I'd been paying so much attention to his face, and I'd not noticed his hand drop below the table. "You keep your hands right where I can see them."

I can assure you I made no sudden moves. We stared at each other for a while longer until I broke the silence.

"Jesus Christ. You killed Brandon Gullick."

"You don't know a goddamned thing."

Pieces clicked into place. It was Lannigan who had searched my truck. How the hell else would he have come up with the name of Norman Blake, unless he'd seen it on a CD in my F-150? Blake was very well known and respected among bluegrass and folk fans, but hardly a household name otherwise. He certainly would not be known to someone who scoffed at "hillbilly music."

And it probably had been Lannigan who had fired those shots in the dark while I was fending off Donny's friends.

Sometimes, I feel like an idiot.

I shrugged, trying to play it cool and buy myself some time for a miracle. "I know you didn't drive down here just now. I know you didn't tell anyone else about me finding Donny Blackmon. I know you decided to pull a gun on me. Jesus, man, just the evidence I've noticed in the last few hours is enough to convince me you are hiding something, and what the hell else could it be? I thought you just wanted money. Christ."

I was talking quietly. I did not want the guy who had his finger on the trigger of a gun aimed at my stomach to worry about the MAGA guys or the cute couple with all the kids overhearing my accusations.

But I kept talking. "You dragged Gullick out there to the farm and killed him. Did Donny see you?"

"You don't know a goddamned thing." It was like he was on a loop, stuck on repeat. "Not a goddamned thing."

"I know you are wondering if you can get by with plugging me right now, here at Mickie D's, in broad daylight, and how you'd explain to your superiors why you shot me, why you are in Pike County, and all that exciting stuff. If you have any brains at all, and I think you do, you are also wondering who else I might have told about you not raising the alarms after I called you. Have you considered that blowing a fucking hole through me might just confirm my hypothesis to any cops I talked to?"

At that moment, I deeply regretted my decision to keep my thoughts to myself when I talked to Detective Scott Baxter. I need to get one of those crystal ball things, so I can see what's coming at me before it slams me in the face.

Lannigan grinned. "I can think of dozens of reasons a cop might shoot a guy," he said.

"Sure," I answered. I grinned, too. Not because I felt great about my situation, of course. It was more because I didn't want Lannigan to know how screwed I felt. "But can you think of any that might explain why you shot a specific guy who told the cops he thought you dragged Brandon Gullick to a notorious cop hater's farm so you could frame Donny Blackmon for Gullick's murder?" I had not told anybody any of those things, of course, but I was playing poker and chicken at the same time. "I really don't think planting a gun or some coke on my body is going to help you out here, Jim."

Again, we stared at one another. But he was sweating more now.

"I think we're going to walk out of here," he said. "Nice and slow."

"I like it here," I said. "I'm thinking about talking with the MAGA guys, maybe asking them why they vote the way they do. Maybe I can sell a piece to the *New York Times*. They love that shit. What do you think?"

"I hate a smart-ass," he muttered.

"Was Brandon a smart-ass? Is that why you killed him? Or did he know something you didn't want known? You been stealing drug evidence? Getting a little action from the girls in exchange for not pressing charges? What else have you done, Lannigan?"

He didn't flinch. "Hands on your head, fingers locked. Stand up," Lannigan ordered. "Slow. Don't draw any attention to yourself." As he said it, his left hand grabbed my coffee cup. He placed it on the seat beside him. So much for me snatching that up and splashing his face full of the superheated lava that McDonald's calls coffee.

I stood, slowly. So did he. His gun was out in the open now. It was a Sig Sauer P320. That would make a pretty big goddamned mess, especially at this range.

"Ed Runyon, I am arresting you on charges of homicide," he said, loud enough for others to hear this time. So that would be his play.

Arrest me, cuff me, take me out of here, and then kill me on some quiet country road. There were plenty of those in Pike County.

If I fought back here, he'd just shoot me and say I resisted arrest. The witnesses probably would back him up on that. He'd have to come up with some plausible reason for trying to arrest me, of course, but he could deal with that later. His more immediate worry, the fact that I was alive and knew he'd killed Gullick, would be eliminated.

Hell, he probably was hoping I'd try something stupid. He probably couldn't wait.

There were other reasons for me to keep my cool and not throw an elbow in his face. A tussle here might get an employee or one of the restaurant patrons shot by a stray bullet.

So, I complied.

"Over to the window."

I went where he told me to go.

"I assume you know the position," he whispered. I did. I leaned against the big plate-glass window, hands high and spread wide against the glass, feet back and away and spread wide. His gun dug into my back. He found my Heckler and Koch VP9 holstered behind me and tucked beneath my shirt. He took that.

Then his free hand reached up and clamped a handcuff on my left wrist. He pulled that arm down and twisted it behind me. If I let his plan run its course, he'd have me helpless within seconds. Once he took me out of the restaurant, he'd drive me out into the boondocks and that would be it. Lights out. No more nights by the fire, no little Eds or Lindas running around in the farmhouse.

I kind of wished the MAGA guys and the fine family and the McDonald's employees would all just scatter, which would be a rational reaction when someone has drawn a gun, but I could see their reflections in the glass and they seemed to be just enjoying the show. If I fought back here, I'd just get people killed.

My only ace card here was the fact there was no goddamned way Lannigan was going to call for backup, at least not until I was dead and he could control the narrative. It meant I had a little time to think. Probably. Mental calculations aren't easy to make when there is a gun against your spine.

"You don't have to do this, Lannigan." I said it quietly.

He put the gun to the back of my head, and that made thinking even more difficult. I wondered if I'd see the glass in front of my face shatter as the bullet exited my forehead. "Shut the fuck up," he muttered.

I shut the fuck up.

Lannigan pulled my free hand down and finished cuffing me.

I decided to get cocky. Hell if I know why. "Don't forget to read me my rights, asshole."

"Fuck you," he whispered. Then, one hand grabbing my chained wrists and the other pushing the gun between my shoulders, he started to march me out.

The MAGA guys actually clapped. Maybe I look like a liberal.

Once we were outside and headed toward Lannigan's SUV, I considered my options. They boiled down to two. I could do something drastic right now while we were in the middle of Waverly, with witnesses nearby walking between their vehicles and the pizza place and the shops in the adjacent shopping plaza. Or, I could let Lannigan kill me.

A Waverly police cruiser rolling slowly through the parking lot was the decisive factor.

I pretended to stumble, let Lannigan get just a tad closer to me than was prudent on his part, then rammed my head backward as hard as I could. Judging from the impact, I caught him squarely in the face.

It's a miracle his gun did not go off, but a smack in the face can make a man forget his intentions for a split second.

He lost his grip on the cuffs, and I ran as hard as I could toward a tiny Ford Fiesta parked nearby. The nice thing about Ford Fiestas is that they are not very big, and I spend a good deal of time running on uneven terrain around a large farm pond to stay fit. Tuck makes fun of me for running there instead of on a nice track or a perfectly smooth road, but I think my choice of running terrain improves my reflexes and conditioning.

I was about to find out if they had improved enough.

I launched myself over the vehicle as Lannigan got off a shot. I don't know where the bullet went, but it didn't go through me. My landing on the other side of the car was not graceful, and all of my bruises suddenly reminded me of their presence. But I was still alive.

I had rolled over the car and landed on my back, abusing my cuffed arms in the process, but I was nonetheless able to get to my feet and dive behind a pickup. It was more of an awkward stumble than a dive, to be honest, but I managed it. Few things motivate me like the thought of bullets in my back.

Lannigan's next salvo shattered a car window. Glass rained around me, and I rolled beneath another vehicle. I could not tell if I'd been cut by the window shards, and I did not have time to check. I had other problems.

People screamed nearby. And then, mercy of mercies, I heard a siren. Not a distant wail, either, but the brief, tentative sound of a siren being fired up for only a second or two—the way cops do when they are already there and just want to get your attention. The officers in the patrol car were paying attention. Hallelujah.

I peeked from my hidey-hole under the van and saw the police vehicle stop. Two sets of feet hit the pavement. I heard a cop shout, "Police! Freeze!"

I heard running footsteps. I guessed that was Lannigan. I seriously doubted he wanted to stick around and explain to the Waverly police just why he'd tried to kill me.

I heard the other cop yell, "Freeze! Police!"

Then a woman chimed in, yelling from somewhere nearby. "There's a man under that truck! I saw him!"

One officer started to chase Lannigan. The other turned toward my hiding place. Then he took cover and ordered me to emerge, slowly, with my hands showing.

I complied, to the extent that I could. "I'm cuffed," I said, rolling onto my stomach so that he could confirm that for himself. Shelly had told me once about a Columbus officer who had gone into a farmhouse after a reported break-in. The man inside claimed he was the homeowner, and that his hands were bound behind his back. Then the asshole told the officer which way the perps had run, and whipped his hands to the front once the officer glanced away. He'd been concealing a pistol. Fortunately, it was a shitty pistol that misfired. The officer's gun had worked just fine.

Anyway, police work is dangerous, and I couldn't blame this guy for being cautious.

"Get up slow," the officer said, still pointing a weapon at me.

It wasn't easy to get to my feet with my arms bound behind me, but I managed it.

The officer kept his weapon aimed at my chest while he called the station on his personal radio. "One subject in custody. Another still at large." I could not make out the reply he got. Once he'd done that, he yelled, "Anyone hurt? Anyone hit?"

Nobody yelled for help or rushed forward with gaping wounds.

The other officer returned. "He got between some vehicles in the other lot, then to the trees back there. Could've gone six different ways." He aimed his gun at me, too. "Hands where I can see them!"

"I am cuffed," I repeated, turning very slowly so he could see that, too. "I'm Ed Runyon, a private investigator. The man who ran is a police detective from Ambletown, named Jim Lannigan, and I believe he killed Officer Brandon Gullick there a few months ago. I can show you his vehicle, and I know what hotel he checked into this morning."

One of them read me my rights.

CHAPTER THIRTY-ONE

THE NEXT HOUR was chaos.

I got hauled to the Waverly Police Department, where two detectives and a sergeant from the Pike County Sheriff's Office asked me a lot of questions. Cops had been dispatched to search Lannigan's hotel room and vehicle, and probably my truck. The sheriff's sergeant, named Paul Seltz, occasionally stepped out of the interview room to bellow at people and have them call Ambletown PD, the Mifflin County SO, the Ohio Highway Patrol, and anyone else he could think of who might be able to confirm the things I was telling him. A pair of helicopters were sent to circle the area around the Mud Run Bluegrass Festival. And everyone was bitching about not letting goddamned reporters get wind of anything until they had a handle on what was going on.

They had removed my cuffs, cleaned and bandaged some fresh scrapes on my arms, and given me a cup of black coffee. It was much better than the stuff I'd left unfinished at McDonald's.

The next time Seltz returned to the interview room, he handed me his phone. "Detective Baxter at Mifflin County SO would like a word, and he is not too pleased."

I took the phone. "Hey, Bax, buddy, how are you?"

"Damn it, Ed! You had your hands on the guy everybody in this state is looking for and you decided you needed to check a few things out before telling me? Is that what I am understanding here? Are you fucking kidding me?"

Angry Bax did not bother with weirdly cryptic mixed metaphors, it seemed.

"Look, I should have told you, but there's a bright side, right? I think we know who really killed Brandon Gullick."

"And about that, damn it, there's another damned thing you needed to tell me. You can't go after a man like that on your own, Ed."

"In my defense, I didn't come to suspect that until he already had a gun aimed at my belly button."

Bax moved the phone away from his face, apparently, because all of his swearing sounded far away for a few seconds. When his voice became distinct again, he was a trifle calmer. "You could have got yourself killed. And we still don't know that Lannigan killed anyone."

"Maybe you don't know, but I am pretty damned convinced. Bax, he wouldn't have drawn on me if he'd kept the news about Donny to himself just so he could claim a reward. I mean, bounty hunting isn't good, but he could've tried to talk his way past that, you know. 'Hey, sorry, I got carried away. I just wanted to be the one to find the man and avenge our brother officer. I'll fly right from now on,' something like that. But, nope, he decided to plug a PI. He was going to kill me, Bax."

"Jesus. OK, I believe you. Do you think him and Donny killed Brandon together? Maybe he's trying to tie up loose ends, worried Donny will get caught and talk?"

I thought about that for a second. "I doubt it. The way Blackmon went underground, it doesn't seem he intends to talk. And he hates cops, anyway, right? Why the hell would he work with a cop on anything?" I tumbled it around in my mind. More thoughts, swirling like crows in the mist.

"Here's what I think," I finally said. "I think Lannigan got Brandon out to Donny's farm somehow. Maybe caught up with him on his morning run, maybe ambushed him. Chloroformed him, stuffed him into a car, and drove him out there. And he killed him there, figuring everyone in the world would blame Donny."

Bax was thinking hard. "So, then, there was a struggle at the barn, though. Gullick got hit in the head, remember."

"Yeah," I answered. "That's weird. Maybe Gullick wakes up from the chloroform quicker than Lannigan thought. I don't know."

"Maybe." I heard Bax cough. "So Donny runs out of fear he'd get the blame."

"No, no, no," I answered. "He didn't just run, he dropped everything and vanished in an instant. And why, assuming Lannigan is our killer, would he be so eager to chase Donny down? And apparently eager to kill him?"

"Shit, Ed. Shit, shit, shit. You think Donny saw Lannigan?"

"Bingo," I replied. "Maybe he saw Lannigan before or after the fact; maybe he even witnessed the deed. And that would explain Donny's behavior. If he knows Lannigan—a cop, remember, and Donny doesn't trust cops any more than I trust gas station egg salad—if he knows Lannigan killed Brandon, and if Lannigan knows that Donny knows, well . . ."

"There's Lannigan's motive for going after Donny so hard. Jesus, Ed, it all makes sense. Except, what's Lannigan's motive for killing Brandon?"

"No idea," I said. "But there are some avenues for investigation now that we have another suspect besides Blackmon. First, if Lannigan is the killer, then he got Donny's gun somehow. Amy says Donny might have sold it."

"We've been all over Donny's computer inside and out," Bax said. "And Donny ran without taking time to wipe anything. Nobody through email or his website asked about buying that gun."

I laughed. "I doubt Lannigan is stupid enough to have reached out in any way that would have left a trace. This is all sounding very premeditated. He knows what the police can do, right?"

"Right."

"So maybe a gun show. Ask all the local gun show regulars if they remember seeing Lannigan at a show. Maybe they even saw him buy something from Donny."

"We already asked around with those guys, trying to see if they recall Donny selling that gun. None did. Of course, they're a tight bunch and not overly fond of cops asking about gun purchases and whatnot."

I started pacing. "I know, Bax. I know you did your due diligence, but you didn't have any other suspects besides Donny at the time, right?"

He blew out a gush of air. "That there is true."

"So, ask again and show Lannigan's photo around."

"Absolutely. We'll do that. Still don't have a motive for Lannigan, though."

"True, but until a couple of minutes ago we didn't really have a reason to look for one. But you guys have all talked with Amble-town cops, right? Any of them say anything about Lannigan and Brandon?"

"No," he said. "Hell, they only worked together a few months before Brandon got killed."

I stopped pacing. "Lannigan won't answer his wife's calls."

"Huh?"

"A couple of times, I've seen it. He just lets it ring, and he gets an ugly look when she calls, too. For a while, I thought Lannigan was just after the Blue Fury money, figuring he'd get soaked in a divorce. But . . . maybe she's the motive."

"You thinking an affair? Her and Brandon?"

"I don't know, maybe. Lannigan told me she was teaching at the college."

"Yeah."

"So Brandon Gullick taught self-defense classes at the college."

"Shit."

"So check and see if she signed up for his class," I suggested. "Or if they ever met up for lunch in the cafeteria or coffee in the teachers' lounge. Did they teach on the same days, stroll across campus holding hands, meet up in the library stacks, anything like that."

"Yeah, yeah. I got it. Jesus, Ed, I hate the idea of a cop killing another cop."

"Yeah. Me, too."

"I'll get guys going to check all that shit on our end. I am coming down there fast as a split log." He must really have calmed down. He was back to the folksy nonsensical metaphors. "Any idea where Lannigan would go next?"

"Far from me, I hope, but finding him is your job, not mine. I'm going to find Donny."

Bax scoffed. "Ed, if we pin the Gullick murder on Lannigan, Donny will come out of hiding, won't he?"

I had read Donny Blackmon's blog, met some of his friends, and stared into his wife's eyes. "Bax, this dude isn't going to believe a damned thing he sees in the news. He'll think it's all a trap."

"Even if he saw Lannigan commit the murder?"

I sighed. "We don't know that for sure, that's just speculation. But yeah, he'll just suspect it's all a ruse, you know? He's not likely to believe the cops are really looking to pin a murder on one of their own. He's going to approach that like these guys who refuse to get the vaccine because it's all a government plot. Reason and evidence is not going to work."

"Maybe, Ed." He paused a few seconds. "You be careful. Donny ain't the only one Lannigan wants to kill."

"Don't I know it. Thanks, Bax."

CHAPTER THIRTY-TWO

WHEN WAVERLY'S FINEST dropped me off at my truck, you can be damned sure I checked the cab and the bed to make sure Lannigan wasn't hiding there, waiting to shoot me with my own gun.

He wasn't.

In another bit of luck, I was happy to see no one had stolen my phone, sitting right there on the seat in plain sight. Not sure that would have been the case in Columbus or Cleveland, but while Waverly had way more traffic lights than little old Jodyville's one, it apparently was safe to leave things in a vehicle for a while. Safer than having lunch at McDonald's with a murderous Ambletown cop, anyway, so I guess the lesson is keep your guard up no matter where you are.

I rolled out of the lot and tried to decide what my next move would be. I remembered checking for free meals at churches and such, but I'd had no narrow focus at the time, and it had quickly seemed fruitless. But one thing I knew for sure was that Donny Blackmon had been in Pike County last night, and it was at least plausible that he'd tried to get a bite to eat here at some point. So I figured I'd start there.

I was about to call Linda when Shelly returned my call from earlier.

"Hi, Shelly."

"Hey, cowboy. I hear you got your mitts on America's most wanted?"

"Close, but no cigar. Did that hit the news already?"

"No, Ed, but cops talk shop, and that's kind of a hot topic."

"Did you ever talk shop with a cop named Jim Lannigan?"

"Yeah. Know him, don't much like him. He throws around words like bitch and slut a bit too freely for my taste."

"In reference to his wife?"

"Erin? Not just her, but, yeah, he's pretty foul-mouthed about her."

I filled Shelly in on my suspicions.

"Damn, Ed."

"I know. Cops are keeping a lid on it for now. Not sure how long they'll be able to do that. Shots fired today, and cop choppers flying over the green fields of Pike County, some roadblocks set up, all that."

"I'll keep an eye out for your pretty face on the nightly news," Shelly said.

"I hope that doesn't happen. I almost think I'd prefer to have a gun aimed at me again to a camera. Tell me what you know about Lannigan."

"I know Erin Lannigan went up to work in Ambletown ahead of Jim, by at least a few weeks. He never stopped bitching about it. It made him kind of surly."

"Well, that fits with my suspicions."

"I do not know much of anything else, though. Like I said, I mostly avoided him. I'll ask around, see if anyone knows anything. I'll let you know what I learn, either way."

"Thanks, Shelly."

"You keep careful. Have you talked to Linda since you got shot at?"

"Been busy."

"Well, get unbusy and call that girl."

"Aye aye, boss. Talk to you later."

I called Linda, and she answered right away. "Hey, good-looking. Did you find your guy?"

"No," I told her. "I got shot at."

"What!"

"You haven't looked at the news today, have you?"

"Are you OK?"

"Yes. I got shot at, but not hit. I have some scrapes, cuts, and bruises. We always called them abrasions, lacerations, and contusions in police reports, you know? But I can just call them scrapes, cuts. and bruises now that I'm my own boss."

"Ed, shut up and get home to me now."

"Sorry, hon. I have not found Donny yet." I explained the details briefly as I pulled into the lot at the Ameristay. I figured I'd get a room, a shower, and a nap. No way was Lannigan coming back here, so I figured it would be safe.

"Ed, Donny is probably long gone by now, right? You told me a million times how careful he is."

"Yeah, but the new trail starts here, and it's the only real grist for the mill I've had on this case, so I'm going to stay and see what I can dig up."

I could hear the hard exhalation on the other end of the phone call. "Ed, you keep an eye out, and if you see Lannigan, you just shoot first."

"Can't. He's got my gun."

"Damn it, Ed, this is not funny."

"I know, I know. I'll be fine. Lannigan probably is trying to pull a disappearing act like Donny did. We can't connect all the dots yet, but we know where some of the dots are, and Lannigan knows that. There's no walking this thing back for him, really. His only good option is to try to get as far away from here as fast as possible. But we'll get him."

"Before he gets you, all right?"

"Yes, dear. I love you."

"I love you, too. Find your guy and get home so I can take care of you."

"Will do."

CHAPTER THIRTY-THREE

THE CHURCH OF God's Holy Word, a recently erected pole barn on Clines Chapel Road in the middle of Nowhere, Ohio, was the seventh or eighth church I visited that late Sunday afternoon. Pastor J. C. Danforth was very glad to see me.

"Evening services don't start for another hour, but I'll be happy to make you a cup of coffee and chat in the meantime, Mister . . ."

"Runyon, Ed Runyon. I'm a private investigator, Reverend Danforth, and I'm—"

"I prefer Pastor Joe, if you don't mind," he said.

"OK, sure, Pastor Joe. Anyway, I am looking for a man, in his forties, thin in the face but broad shoulders, bald, tattoos on his head, may have showed up here anytime in the last few months looking for food, shelter, spiritual advice, anything like that."

Pastor Joe, a tall man with a face that reminded me of Tom Cruise for reasons I could not quite come to grips with, looked very concerned. "Well, I, um, I'm not sure . . ."

Poker was not his game. His eyebrows had gotten higher with each descriptive word I'd used regarding Donny Blackmon.

"Sir, I assure you, he's not in any kind of legal trouble or anything like that." That was a lie, of course, since he officially was still a suspect in a cop's homicide, but I had a job to do. "His family hired me to convey some important family matters to him, that's all."

Pastor Joe, whether it was a result of my amazing portrayal of trustworthiness or some innate ability on his part to judge character, decided to believe me. "Well, it sounds like you could be talking about Eric Cohen," he said. "He showed up at our free meal—we do that once a week, all year, at the American Legion post in Waverly—maybe three weeks ago. Tired and hungry, he was. Obviously in trouble. Pastors learn to recognize the signs, unfortunately. But Eric, bless him, insisted on paying back, you know? He did not want to just accept our sliced ham and beans and cornbread. He took up a position on the line and helped serve others. And he wanted to work, too, although . . ."

"Under the table?" I nodded as I said it.

"Well, yes," Pastor Joe said. "He didn't see why Uncle Sam should get a cut of anything he earned and . . . frankly, I agree with him."

"None of that matters to me," I said. "I don't always like what the government does with my money, either." Tax money went into my own paychecks once upon a time, but the pastor did not need to know that.

"Amen," he said. He winked at me, as though the two of us were in on some great secret.

I leaned a little closer. "Did you find him work?"

"I directed him to a man who is often looking for manual labor, yes. A member of our church."

"Can you tell me who you referred him to?"

Pastor Joe thought about it for a moment, then decided to tell me. "Mark Babcock," he said. "He has a large farm, and a lot of timber, and he's always looking for men, or teens, too, who can bail hay, move logs, load trucks, all that."

Mark Babcock was the name of the man who hosted the Mud Run Bluegrass Festival, according to the tie-dyed hippie announcer guy. Connections were starting to come together.

"Do you know if Mr. Babcock hired Eric?"

"He did. They came together for our community meals a couple of times. Mark does not need the food, obviously, but he comes in now and then and helps serve. He buys a lot of the food, too. He's a good man. The last couple of times he did that, Eric was with him, and Eric helped serve the meals, too. Mark spoke highly of him, called him a good worker. I appreciated that, you know, because, well, not everyone I refer to Mark is willing to work hard. They usually stick with it for a day or two days then drift away."

I nodded. "That's a shame. When was the last time you saw Eric?"

Pastor Joe gazed at the ceiling. "I don't think he's been in for a few days, probably five at least. He does not attend church services."

"Do you think he's still working for Mr. Babcock?"

He shrugged. "Could be, I suppose. I haven't seen either man in a while. Mark attends church, but not regularly. He is a very busy man, you know, with a lot going on. I've tried to encourage him to attend more often, of course, for his benefit and for the benefit of others here, because I think an example of a hardworking man might inspire some of these younger people to pay their dues, you know. No one wants to work, it seems."

I jumped in with another question before he could elaborate. "Can you tell me where Mr. Babcock lives? Do you have his phone number?"

"He would not want me to give out his number," Pastor Joe said, apologetically. "I wouldn't be comfortable doing that. He's a very private man."

"I understand. Can you share his address?"

Pastor Joe smiled. "Everyone knows that," he said. "He owns a big chunk of land. There was a music festival out there this weekend, the Mud Run Bluegrass Festival. Banjos and high-pitched singing, from what I understand. Not my sort of thing, but it's nice of him to open up his farm like that for those who enjoy the twangy music."

I already knew the way to the farm, but I let Pastor Joe give me directions anyway.

"I appreciate your time, sir." I handed him one of my cards. "If you think of anything that might help, please give me a call, day or night. His family is very eager to get in touch with him."

He nodded. "I'll pray that all works out well, Mr. Runyon."

"Thanks. When is the next community meal, by the way?"

"Noon to four, Tuesday. Ham and beans, with cornbread. Do you plan to come by?" He looked hopeful.

"I just might," I said. "I do like beans and cornbread. Thanks for doing that, by the way."

"A lot of people need help these days." He shrugged. "We do what we can."

I left the church and checked my truck for a hidden killer before I climbed in.

CHAPTER THIRTY-FOUR

I WAS STILL trying to decide whether to give Bax the new information I had about Donny Blackmon's possible whereabouts when my phone buzzed. Believe it or not, the caller was Jerry Spence.

"Hey, Jerry. Looks like you got your phone back. Don't start sending threats to people who might kick your ass, OK?"

"Yeah," he said. "Look, about the threats . . ."

"I don't care about those, as long as you stop doing shit like that. I have to admit, though, that you're the last person I expected a call from."

He laughed. "Yeah, well, there's still work to do, right? And finding Donny could be lucrative. I think I am close by, honestly. I heard about some of the activity in Pike County and it sounds like maybe cops are closing in on our guy. I heard you were on the scene. Are you?"

"I'm not looking for a partner, Jerry."

"Sure," he said. "I'm not easy to work with, I know, and, well, anyway. But . . . I have a line on somebody who might be helping Donny hide. I thought maybe we could brainstorm, pool our talents, and maybe find the guy before the cops do. Or any bounty hunters. I mean, there's still a chance at some good money here."

I had no real desire to encounter Jerry Spence again, but if he had any legitimate information on Mark Babcock or anyone else, I wanted to hear it. "Who's helping him?"

"No, no, no, Ed." He laughed. "I want an exchange of information. If I just hand you what I know, I'm out of leverage, right?"

"Right," I said. "I'll just wing it without you, then."

"Don't hang up." He muttered a little under his breath. "Look, you don't like me, I get it. I haven't given you any reason to like me. In fact, I've given you reasons not to like me."

"Me and every other PI in the state," I reminded him.

"And I feel bad about it, I really do. I want to make amends. I think we can help each other out, and there's enough reward money, hell, we can split that. If I'm right about the guys helping Donny, it might not be so easy getting to him. You'll be glad you have help. Of course, I could be wrong. Maybe what you know can help verify what I know, and vice versa. Anyway, you can listen to what I have and share what you have, and when we're all done you can decide if we work together or not, OK? But we'll both have more info. More info is good, right?"

I sighed. "Well, Jerry, my friend Tuck tells me the only things we mere humans have of any real value are the people we love, and our time here on Earth. You are not a person I love . . ."

He laughed. "God, I know that."

". . . so you better not be wasting my time. Where are you?"

"I could use a bite. There's a Bob Evans on the north end of Waverly."

"Yeah, I've seen it. I could go for some biscuits and gravy myself. I'll be there in ten minutes."

"See you there."

CHAPTER THIRTY-FIVE

As I HEADED into town, I considered all the reasons I should call Bax, or the Pike County Sheriff's Office, or some other legitimate law enforcement agency to tell them what I'd learned from Pastor Joe. Mark Babcock, the driving force behind the Mud Run Bluegrass Festival, apparently had struck up a relationship with Donny Blackmon, previously the chief suspect in the murder of Ambletown Police Officer Brandon Gullick.

The local police likely had some good information about Mark Babcock. All I knew was that Babcock made money from farming and timber, hired cheap labor, attended church from time to time, and helped with the community meals. The Pike County Sheriff's Office, on the other hand, probably knew a lot about the man and the lay of his farm. They could reference topographical maps, identify access points, check known associates, and do a million other things more efficiently than I could with my cell phone from my truck.

They also were expending a lot of resources in the manhunt. Helicopters cost money to fly. Officers were being paid overtime. All of those resources could be very useful in rounding up the man. If Donny still was hiding somewhere on the Babcock farm, there would be a huge advantage in having an army of peace officers to surround the place.

So, you see, my brain said I should call in the forces of the law.

Of course, my brain has two hemispheres and, if you ask Tuck, those two hunks of gray cells do not always function at an optimal level. I started thinking of reasons I should not call on the long arm of the law.

As far as I was concerned, Donny was no longer a suspect in the death of Brandon Gullick. But the machinery of law enforcement seldom makes snap decisions, and there likely still were plenty of cops who were not in on the latest news in this case. Calling in the cops could be little different from calling in a bunch of bounty hunters. In the minds of most cops, Donny probably still was the prime suspect. Cops in Ambletown and Mifflin County could be expected to keep up on case details and probably had been briefed on the latest developments. Other cops? They probably got most of their information from scuttlebutt and social media. All they knew was that Donny Blackmon hates cops, was accused of killing a cop, and had been the focus of a manhunt for months.

Some of them might just shoot him on sight.

And then, of course, there could be actual bounty hunters out there. Organizing a bunch of cops would take time, and during that time information could leak. That could result in guys who wanted that Blue Fury cash descending on Pike County, and that could get Donny killed. Or it could get someone else killed. That someone else, potentially, could be me. I'd recently spent a very unpleasant night listening to a bunch of good ol' boys arguing over the best way to kill me and dispose of my remains. Do you think I wanted a reprise of that?

Hell no.

By the time I pulled into the Bob Evans parking lot, I'd decided to delay my decision until I'd heard what Jerry Spence had to say. I saw him standing near the restaurant door, next to a handicap signpost that looked as skinny as he did. He waved, I waved back, and then I parked.

As soon as I stepped out of my truck, I felt the cold touch of a gun muzzle at the back of my head.

"Hello, Runyon." It was, of course, Jim Lannigan's voice. "No tricks this time. I got nothing else to lose, goddamn it."

CHAPTER THIRTY-SIX

I WAS MANHANDLED into the back of Spence's bland Toyota before I had a chance to react, and there was no police car traveling nearby to help me out this time.

Lannigan ended up sitting beside me, my own gun aimed at my face. "You're a slippery son of a bitch, Runyon. Keep still, or I'll shoot you right here. And keep your hands on your lap."

I nodded. It was a lame response, I know, but it was the best I could do in the moment. A few seconds later, though, I came up with, "Run out of chloroform this time, Jim?"

"Shut up."

I was still screwed, of course, but I felt a little better.

Spence got in behind the wheel. In the rearview mirror, I could see his bruised face. He smiled around a cigarette he hadn't lit yet. "Hello, Ed."

"Fuck you, Jerry."

Spence found a lighter somewhere on the seat beside him and lit up. Once he exhaled, he looked up to the mirror again. "This is for the problems you caused me," he said.

"Sure," I replied. "Why should you take any responsibility yourself, right? Mr. Innocent."

Lannigan cleared his throat. "Shut up and drive, Jerry."

"Yes, sir."

Spence guided the Toyota out of the parking lot and turned north on a two-lane road. "Let's go for a ride."

I assessed the situation, looking for some brilliant maneuver to get me out of this mess. I sat directly behind the driver, with Lannigan to my right. The detective was breathing hard and sweating. His face was scratched, possibly by tree limbs as he ran through woods to avoid capture. And his nose was dark and swollen, probably from the impact of my skull. His hand was steady enough on the gun, though. I decided any sudden move from me—elbow in Lannigan's face, snatch at the pistol, whatever—was going to make that goddamned thing go off. And Lannigan was right, I'd left him with nothing left to lose. He was on the run, and even if he shot me right here and made a big bloody mess in Spence's car, it would not really make his situation much worse. He was only taking me elsewhere so he could kill me in a more convenient spot, somewhere he could leave my corpse while he made his escape to God knows where.

If I forced him, though, he'd just shoot me right here.

Spence did not seem under duress at all. Indeed, he was almost downright jovial, smiling whenever he caught my face in his mirror.

We soon were beyond the city limits, traveling on a winding road with mostly fields and trees to our right and the occasional farmhouse uphill to our left. There was still plenty of summer daylight left, but that gave me no real reason for hope. This looked like country where you could get out of sight quickly, sunshine or not. I didn't think Lannigan would wait until nightfall to take my life.

"You really fucked me, Runyon," Lannigan muttered. "You really did."

"You were fucked anyway," I answered. "Marriage is a mess, nobody likes you, you smell bad."

"Shut up."

I did. In the silence, I connected dots. Spence apparently had been making money as a snitch for Columbus cops. Lannigan had been an unpopular Columbus cop. Now here they were, teaming up to kill me and hide my remains somewhere in beautiful rural Ohio.

I decided talking some more could hardly make my situation worse. "So, Jim. You the one blackmailing Jerry? Did you promise Spence you'd end the blackmail if he helped you out? Is that what you've got on him?"

Spence's smile disappeared. "You fucking don't worry about my problems, Ed. You got your own."

I actually laughed. "Fuck, Jerry. This whole thing is about getting rid of witnesses, you dumbass. He's going to kill you when—"

The impact was lightning, gun butt against skull. I was blinded, but my mind could envision an impact crater in my head. Lannigan had put some muscle into it. After a few seconds of intense pain, I became aware I was shouting a torrent of curse words.

"Don't worry, Jerry," Lannigan said. "He's just trying to play you against me. You are a useful guy, Jerry, and I'm going to need that, right? You keep being useful, you got nothing to worry about."

I, on the other hand, had plenty to worry about. I could feel blood oozing into my right ear.

I had learned one thing, though. Lannigan could be angered, and angry men make mistakes. I decided to risk another swat on the head.

"Why'd you kill Gullick? Was he fucking your wife?"

He hit me again, all right, but not with the gun as I'd hoped. It was a left jab, with plenty behind it even though he'd had little distance to work with. It caught my jaw and turned my head. It was a nice view once my eyes cleared. I saw a road going off to our left, and a nice big old barn in the distance. I wondered if that was where I would die.

"Turn here," Lannigan commanded. Spence tossed his mostly spent smoke out the window and complied, then Lannigan addressed me again. "I know what you are trying to do, Runyon. It won't work."

"You don't have to do this, Jim," I said. I hoped I didn't sound like I was begging. "Killing me does not solve any of your problems."

"It'll solve one of them," he said. "You fucked me hard, and this is about payback." He laughed a bit, on the borderline of hysteria. "Killing you won't actually make my problems any worse, you know? How could anything get worse?" That brought more quiet, yet manic, laughter.

"You should just run, Jim. Just run." I couldn't tell if he was listening to me or not.

He stopped laughing, though. "Jerry, that barn up there, looks like it'll work. Let's check it out."

"Sure."

The road meandered a bit between barbed wire fences until we came to a dirt lane that led to the barn about fifty yards away. Spence paused the vehicle, and my captors looked around a bit. So did I. There was not a single other barn, home, vehicle, or human being within sight. There was no sign of any work being done at the barn. We could see nothing but rolling pasture dotted with copses and cows, and a few sparrows darting about.

If I was looking for a place to kill a guy and dump his body, I'd sure call this a contender. A spy satellite might witness my murder, but no one else would.

"Let's check it out," Lannigan said, and Spence turned the Toyota up the dirt lane.

The barn was falling apart, held up by rusty nails and some other invisible means. Many dark planks had fallen or split, and the doors had been removed at some point, possibly to decorate somebody's rustic home. Inside, there was a large round metal cage full of hay, so the cows could wander in and eat, and a couple of troughs. I couldn't tell if there was water in them.

Cows looked up from the tall grass as we approached, but they soon lost interest.

"Circle behind it," Lannigan said. He was sweating profusely now, and his eyes had a crazy glaze to them. He was losing it but still giving orders. "If anyone's around, ask for directions to Waverly. Runyon, if you make a peep, I'll kill anyone who hears you."

I believed him.

Spence did as he was told. We saw no one.

"Well, then," Lannigan said. "Let's do this. Like we discussed, Jerry."

"Right."

The car slipped around a bit. I glanced out the window and saw the ground was muddy in places. There had not been rain the last couple of days, but water stood in deep ruts left by a big truck or tractor. I supposed someone had hauled water here for the cows. I supposed cows piss wherever the hell they happen to be standing, too. Anyway, it was a mess.

Spence parked behind the barn. We were now out of view from the road, although gaps in the barn walls might have given someone a glimpse if they tried really hard. Some of the gaps were almost wide enough for Spence to step through.

Spence took something from the glove box and got out of the car. He walked around a bit, put the keys in his pocket, and then turned to face the vehicle.

He was holding a .38-caliber revolver.

"Now," Lannigan said. "You get out, nice and slow."

"I don't think so," I said. "If I'm going to die, I'd just as soon ruin Jerry's car to make sure there is evidence to implicate him in all this."

Spence opened my car door. "Out!"

This put me between two men aiming guns at me, which was not a great place to be, but necessity is the mother of crazy desperate moves, or so they say.

I put a foot outside the car, shouldered my way out while keeping my hands where my captors could see them, then drove myself as hard as I could at Jerry Spence. In college football, I'd have been called for targeting. I aimed the crown of my head right at his bruised face.

He shouted and toppled backward. I stumbled and fell with him, and two guns went off.

I did not feel any sudden holes, but it's possible the pain in my skull from being pistol whipped was distracting me. A little blood trickled into my right eye, but I convinced myself it was from Spence's broken nose.

Lannigan screamed. Spence did, too. I rolled right as hard as I could, toward the barn that was not even able to keep out a stiff breeze, so no way was it going to stop bullets. But my only other choices for cover were cows, and they were running away.

I got to my feet as gunshots rang out behind me. Two distinct weapons, so I had not lucked out and gotten either of my captors to accidentally kill the other. Damn it.

I ran around the barn, stumbling on the uneven, cattle-stomped ground, and hoped to find a miracle on the other side. No such luck.

More shots rang out. I could not simply run for it. The landscape sloped gently away in every direction. That would give two shooters the high ground and leave me in the open. I had not been able to calculate how many shots they'd already expended, but my H&K VP9 had contained fifteen rounds when Lannigan took it from me, and I doubted Spence had emptied his revolver. Even if they were both shitty marksmen, they'd have enough ammo to get the job done.

So I kept going around the barn, reached the space where the doors should have been, and dove inside. I crouched behind one of the troughs. A bullet had pierced it, and water was pouring onto the dirt, straw, and cow shit.

Outside, Lannigan and Spence stopped shooting. I did not risk a look, but I figured they were flashing hand signals, maybe circling the barn. One would go clockwise, the other widdershins. They'd likely meet at the door on opposite sides, and come in blazing, one high and the other low, just like in the movies.

I started looking for a weapon. The best I could do was a pitchfork, standing up in the hay cage. I don't know if you've ever considered the range on a pitchfork, but it's nothing compared to a gun. I was not encouraged, but I grabbed it up. And what the hell, I'd gone into a fight once armed with a bowling ball, and at least the pitchfork had sharp tines. Things were looking up, I told myself.

Now hiding behind the hay and peering through the cracks, I couldn't determine where Lannigan was at all, but I could see Spence. He was moving along the north wall, peeking through the gaps in the barn wood, looking for me.

I listened and heard heavy breathing. I was right. Lannigan was on the south side of the barn. He was smarter than Spence, though, and was not up close to the barn where I could easily discern his position.

They were circling and approaching the entrance from opposite directions.

Once they got to the entrance, of course, they would have me at their mercy. The hay I hid behind was not going to stop bullets, and they could shoot me as many times as they wanted. I'd be leaking blood the way the trough was leaking water.

I tried to get a good grasp on the pitchfork. My hands were sweaty, but the handle was rough-hewn so I wasn't too concerned about it slipping from my hands. I was much more concerned about Jerry Spence's revolver.

After a very brief mental pep talk, which mostly consisted of telling myself it was better to get shot in the face while fighting back than to just wait for death to come and find you cowering, I got to my feet.

Spence was inching closer to the corner, where he'd be only a few steps away from the perfect spot to kill me.

If I was to have any damned chance at all, I had to go now.

I charged the wall, my pitchfork before me like a spear, the tines aligned vertically. I aimed for a gap just a bit wider that Spence's tie. I could just see him beyond it. He was peering inside, looking for me.

His eyes went wide and he raised the gun, poking it through the gap. He'd have been much better off just leaping backward, but not everyone thinks straight when battle is joined.

The pitchfork caught him in the chest before he could squeeze the trigger. The tines sank deep. I'd put all my considerable size and strength behind the blow, but not just so I could drive a farm implement through a guy.

I was hoping this barn was as close to collapse as it looked.

My shoulder hit the wood, and for a moment I was not sure if the loud crack came from my clavicle or the rotted timber. But I went through, throwing splinters and black paint chips everywhere and driving Jerry Spence into the ground, impaled like a vampire. I tripped on him, lost my grip on the pitchfork, and tumbled in a heap of mud, blood, broken wood, and manure.

It all made a hell of a lot of noise.

I rolled onto my stomach and wiped dung from my eyes. Spence had not cried out, but that didn't matter. Lannigan had to have heard me going through the barn wall. The only question was whether he'd come charging to shoot me as quickly as he could, before I could recover, or whether he'd crouch low and wait to assess the situation before he acted. As far as I could tell, that was a fucking coin toss. He was a very desperate man, and you can't tell what a desperate man might do.

I also wondered what the hell I might do. The pitchfork wasn't going to work twice.

I finally spotted Spence's revolver in the muck. I crawled to it and snatched it up. A quick check told me I had two shots left. I figured Lannigan had a lot more.

The gun was covered in mud. I shook it hard and hoped like hell the barrel wasn't clogged.

I got into a crouch, my aim wavering first to one side of the barn, then the other. I had no idea where Lannigan was.

He did not appear in either place.

I rose, and backed away, slowly. I was certain he had a pretty good fix on my position. I had no real way to gauge his.

My heart thumped. Louder—louder—louder. I felt like the killer in Poe's story, wondering why the law officers could not hear the beating of the heart. Surely Lannigan could hear this kick drum in my chest.

Maybe he did.

Lannigan peeked around the corner of the east wall, the one where the barn door was supposed to be. He had a big dark stain on his jeans. He'd been wounded in the left leg, maybe even by Spence's gun during my first desperate attempt to get free. Perhaps I'd had more luck than I'd thought.

I was out of luck now.

Lannigan saw me, took a shot and missed. I shot and thought I got him in the shoulder. It was difficult to tell. He vanished behind the corner quickly.

The weapon I held contained one more bullet.

I decided to try logic and calm discussion, because what the fuck else could I do? "You gain nothing by killing me, Jim!"

No answer.

"Enough people are dead, don't you think?" I moved slowly, and quietly. I did not want to be in the same spot if Lannigan decided to use up more bullets.

"Even if you take me down, Jim, how far can you get? How far do you think you can get?" I took a second to wipe away sweat from my forehead, hoping to keep my eyes clear. My sleeve was a mess, though, so that did not work well.

"Is this the life you want, Jim? On the run? Afraid of everything?"

I thought I heard a sob. He did not answer me, though.

"Let's stop all this, Jim. Come on out, drop the gun, you go lawyer up and explain. Maybe there's more to all this than I know."

A car door slammed, then Lannigan yelled, "Fuck!"

The keys were in Jerry's pocket.

The car door slammed again, and I heard footsteps. Lannigan was running for it, as best as he could. He was not moving well, but he was headed for the road.

I did not risk a long shot. I had just one round left, and Lannigan on the run was not a present danger to me. I did not figure he'd get very far. I could call the cops, tell them where we were, and let them come with helicopters and tactical teams.

I reached for my pocket.

The universe laughed. My phone was in my truck.

I flipped my middle finger at the sky and walked over to Spence's corpse, hoping to find his phone.

The pitchfork handle sticking up from Spence's chest wobbled, like a dowser's rod, before it finally stopped. It was aiming straight up. I figured if Jerry Spence had a soul, it was headed in the other direction.

I found his phone. It had my pitchfork in it.

CHAPTER THIRTY-SEVEN

I FISHED AROUND in Spence's pocket until I found the keys. That was about as pleasant as it sounds. His eyes were wide open over a busted nose that had bled all over his face. He looked surprised.

I guess I'd be surprised to see a guy charging me with a pitchfork, too.

Heading back to the Toyota, I kept watching the road and the tall grass around me. There was no guarantee at all that Lannigan had reached the road and kept going. He could be out there in the tall grass, lying in ambush. So I moved quickly, nearly falling a couple of times on the uneven ground, gun out in front of me ready to fire.

I reached the vehicle unscathed and climbed in. Then I drove Spence's Toyota back to the road. The blood spatters were bigger than I'd expected, and they told me a story. Lannigan had gone right, back the way we'd come. He'd also been hurt worse than I'd realized.

I thought for a while there at the intersection, trying to decide my next move. My brain said to go the other way, find someone with a phone, and call in the troops. They had plenty of firepower and a couple of helicopters not too far from here, looking for Donny Blackmon. All I needed to do was find a phone.

I was, of course, on a lonely country road. There was no telling how long it would take to find someone with a phone, and I was covered in shit and Spence's blood, so I'd have to build in time to convince somebody that I was not an axe murderer or something worse. Lannigan could choose to go off in any direction while I farted around with all that. He could stumble upon someone with a car or truck and take a hostage. Or he could vanish in the woods, maybe eat roots and berries and shit and cup water in his hands to drink from creeks, then stay in the water and go upstream or down, just to throw off any bloodhounds.

Damn, I wished I had some bloodhounds.

Anyway, Lannigan was completely unhinged and possibly feverish. He might do anything to put distance between himself and pursuit, or he might crawl off into the forest and die in some lonely spot where no one would ever find him.

I was not about to let that happen. So I turned right and followed him.

I drove slowly, windows down, one hand on the wheel and one holding Spence's revolver. I'd found no extra ammo on his person or in his vehicle. I still had just one shot.

Lannigan was much better armed, as he had my pistol and probably still had his service weapon, too. He could be hiding somewhere, expecting me to show up. He could emerge from behind a tree or out of a ditch and send the rest of my own goddamned bullets flying through the windshield.

So I moved slowly, looking left and right, ready to stomp on the gas and drive right into the son of a bitch if I had to.

Lannigan was leaving a serious blood trail. Following him was not difficult, but the sun was lowering. If I didn't find him soon, I'd have to get out of the car to be able to spot the blood on the road.

That did not sound fun.

An SUV approached from the opposite direction. I put the gun on the seat beside me, stopped the Toyota, and waved my arm, hoping the driver would stop. He did. He was an older guy with one of those red MAGA hats atop a head full of bushy white and gray hair. He eyed me with suspicion, and I hoped he could not see all of Jerry Spence's blood on my clothes. "Got a problem?"

"Did you see anyone on the road, walking?"

"No, sorry."

"That's OK. Listen. My name is Ed Runyon. I'm a private investigator in pursuit of a fugitive named Jim Lannigan. I want you to drive, get away from here, because he's armed and he's desperate. But call the sheriff. Give them both names, mine and the guy I'm after. Tell them where you are. They'll come running."

He nodded. "OK."

"You got the names?"

"Ed Runyon. Jim Lannigan."

"Bless you, sir. Go!"

He floored it and was gone.

I resumed my slow crawl along the road, gun back in hand. If the SUV driver had not seen my quarry, it was likely that Lannigan had left the road. Not much farther along, the blood spatters went to the left shoulder. I saw a crimson smear on a guardrail.

I pulled Spence's car as far off the road as I could, got out, and ran to cover by a big oak. I expected a hail of bullets, but that didn't happen.

I did not need to be Natty Bumppo to figure out where Lannigan had gone. The landscape rose beyond the bloodstained guardrail, and there was one very fresh scrape in the ground where a shoe had ripped away the soil in an attempt to climb. I scanned some more and noted blood on a maple trunk. There was more blood beyond that.

Lannigan had gone upward. Him and all of his bullets.

Me, a bigger and stronger Barney Fife, had just the one. But up I went.

It was slow going. At times it was steep, and I had to pull myself upward using roots and branches. I paused behind cover, often, and peered through the woods. It gets darker in the woods faster than it does out in the open. That would be a problem for both Lannigan and myself, but he could solve his problem by spraying bullets at me.

I wasn't going to be able to follow his blood trail if it got much darker.

A squirrel skittered along a branch nearby and scared the shit out of me.

I stretched out behind a large fallen oak. I needed to get an idea of how far he'd gotten. I decided to take a risk.

"Lannigan? You need to come out!"

Five shots ripped the trees and underbrush around me. Nothing came close to hitting me, but I knew two things. He had not gotten far, and that had not been the sound of my gun.

He still had his service weapon.

I counted to thirty, then slowly rolled toward the other end of the log, away from where his salvo had flown. "I know you're hurt, Jim! I can get you help!"

This time an anguished scream accompanied the bullets. Six of them. One tore some bark off the oak near me. And he'd fired both weapons that time.

I waited five minutes, hoping he'd come down the hill to see if he'd killed me. Maybe the sound of his movement would give me a clear idea where he was, and I could make my one shot pay off.

Lannigan waited me out, and it got darker.

I climbed over my protective tree trunk, quiet as a ghost, and continued upward.

I heard sobbing.

Sitting behind an outcropping of rock, I found a fallen branch. I reached for it, thinking to toss it aside in hopes I could get Jim to waste more bullets by firing at the sound. Instead, the branch got tangled in the forest growth and made a ridiculous amount of noise. Lannigan fired more shots, all right—five, I think. All of them close.

"Damn you, Runyon!" Four more shots.

"Killing me gets you nothing, Jim." I did not risk a look. Another round zinged off the rock nearby.

"You don't understand," he said. He was sobbing now. "I was good to her! Good to her! And she . . . she . . ."

I figured blunt words would piss him off the most. "She fucked Brandon Gullick."

Four shots in rapid sequence, all from my handgun. I had no idea how many rounds he had left. I had no idea whether he had extra ammo. I had no idea why I was trying to piss off a man with guns.

To get him to waste bullets, my brain said.

"That's just stupid," I muttered to myself.

I stayed under cover, absolutely afraid to move. Shadows stretched among the trees. Birds chirped and chattered somewhere beyond sight. My heart was doing that thing again from Poe's story.

Then, he spoke again. Just a series of incoherent words, between sobs. "That . . . she just . . . I can't . . ."

"Jim! You can tell her, man. You can tell her. Let me get you out of here. We'll get you a doctor, bind up those wounds. You need blood, man. You're in serious, serious trouble."

"Fuck yourself, Runyon!"

That was punctuated by a click.

"Oh, oh, oh."

Another click.

Next came a wail, an ungodly unleashing of fear and terror and mourning.

I risked a look.

Jim Lannigan was seated against an oak, my weapon against his head, pulling the trigger only to produce a series of useless clicks. He was hysterical now.

I crept forward, gun aimed. "Jim. Drop the gun, man. And show me your left hand. Slow."

He raised his left hand, slowly, and dropped the gun it held. His right hand was still trying to blow his brains out.

"Stop that, Jim. Drop the gun."

He looked at me, and clicked the trigger again.

"Jim, stop."

He dropped it. "I'd have gotten her back," he said, his voice raw.

"Toss me your phone. Slowly. Left-handed."

He reached into his pocket, slowly. "I'd have got her back."

"That had better be a phone."

It was.

"Toss it to me," I ordered, calmly. "Then keep your hands where I can see them."

"You fucked me hard, man." He tossed the phone. I kept my aim on him and picked up the phone with my free hand. I hoped to hell there was juice in the battery and that I could get a signal here.

"You fucked me hard. Can't get her back now, can't get . . . anything. Can I? All done. All done. All done."

I spat. "You killed a man, Jim."

He kept muttering while I waited for my call to go through. "Tough fucker," he said. "Woke up. Fought me." Lannigan started to laugh. "Almost kicked my ass." Then the weeping resumed. He was shaking.

Baxter answered the phone. "Hello, Detective Baxter."

"Bax," I said. "It's me."

"Ed?"

"I have Lannigan. He's hurt bad. Bleeding in a couple of spots. We'll need an ambulance, and I don't think I can get him down to the road myself."

"Yeah, we got a call from some guy, says he talked to you. We're already on the way. You'll probably hear the first chopper any second, Ed."

"Look for a dull gray Toyota. We're uphill from that. Not too far, but it's overgrown, won't be easy to bring a stretcher up. But we're going to need one."

"Got it. You OK? You sound out of breath."

"Been very busy," I said. "Got knocked in the head a couple times, shot at a lot but not hit. There's a barn, up the road past where we are. You'll find a guy dead there."

"Jesus, Ed."

"Like I said. I've been busy. Come quick, Bax."

I ended the call.

I kept my aim on Lannigan, just in case he had more surprises. "You know," I said. "If you'd kept your cool at McDonald's, you might have gotten away with it. Jesus, I was stupid. I really did think you were after the reward money. I had no idea you'd killed Gullick until you decided to kill me at McDonald's."

He laughed. It was a bitter sound. "Shit." Then he started crying again.

"That was you at the festival, firing shots in the dark after I found Donny. You tried to kill him then."

Lannigan kept weeping, but he nodded his head.

We sat there as the woods got slowly darker, and then I heard the helicopter.

CHAPTER THIRTY-EIGHT

I SAT ON the open tailgate while a young woman swathed my scrapes and a young man took my blood pressure. The people who tend to my scrapes and cuts seem to get younger every year.

They'd already bandaged the head wound left when Lannigan struck me with his gun, and they'd shined lights at my eyes and asked me to count fingers and recite numbers forward and backward. My head still hurt, but apparently, I'd escaped serious harm.

Jim Lannigan was already on his way to the emergency room.

Detective Scott Baxter stared at me. "You look bad, Ed, like a puppy been in a chicken coop, but I have seen you worse."

I mustered a weak laugh. "Yeah, I'll be OK. Linda's going to make me start selling insurance, though. I don't know how you married guys do this."

He stared at his feet for a moment, then looked me in the eyes. "For one thing, Ed, we don't go charging off into the woods all by ourselves chasing a goddamned gunman. Linda ought to be pissed at you. I'm pissed at you. You should've called in the whole posse, Ed. That's what we're here for."

"Well," I said, shrugging. "I left my phone in my truck when they kidnapped me. And I speared Jerry Spence's phone with a pitchfork."

Baxter shook his head hard. "Still wrapping my head around that. Goddamned pitchfork. I mean . . . holy hell."

I ignored all that. "The only phone left was the one Lannigan carried, and I couldn't get at it because he was shooting at me."

While Bax slowly shook his head and stared at the ground, I looked up into the woods. Flashlights sent beams between tall trunks as officers looked for bullets, footprints, and other clues that could corroborate or falsify my account. They already had Lannigan's gun, my gun, and the one I'd taken from Spence. I figured there was no way they'd find all of the bullets.

Baxter stopped imagining the pitchfork in Jerry Spence's chest and came back to the present moment, very zen-like except he was obviously very pissed off. "There's a farm less than a mile around the bend going the other way from the barn. Somebody there's got a phone."

"Damn," I said. "Should've thought of that."

"I don't know how Linda and Tuck put up with you." He was pacing now.

"They don't always. Sometimes Tuck shorts my order on french fries just because he's mad at me. And Linda steals my fries."

Bax finally grinned. "Tuck's fries are worth stealing."

"Hell yeah."

He came closer once all of my cuts and scrapes had been cleaned up. "We did find a connection between Officer Gullick and Erin Lannigan," Bax said, tapping on his phone. "Have a look." He held his device up so I could see the screen. It was a news article on *Ambletown Live*, a website that tried to pretend it was a newspaper, but it really just featured shiny happy press release stuff. You were never going to find out the sheriff was turning his buddies loose after arrests for disturbing the peace, or that a local politician was suspected of beating his wife, or that the city of Ambletown was being sued over spending tax money on a Nativity display on public property at Christmas. You had to go to a real news website to find out about that stuff.

Ambletown Live, however, did a good job of basic fluff pieces, like the one Bax was showing me. It was a feature story, from a few months back, about self-defense classes offered to women at Ambletown University. The class was taught by local police officer Brandon Gullick.

"Look at the photo," Bax instructed me. I did.

The photo showed a pretty redhead standing over Officer Brandon Gullick, who was lying on his back on a mat after presumably being thrown over the redhead's shoulder. According to the caption, the redhead was Erin Lannigan.

"I'll be damned," I said.

"I already talked to her. She confirmed the affair, and it seemed to me she already half suspected her husband had killed Brandon. She didn't say that, but, well, she did not sound surprised one bit."

I shook my head. "Anything to connect Lannigan to Donny's gun?"

"We have security camera footage of him at three fairground gun shows before the killing," Bax said. "One of our gals found it quick, because she remembered seeing Lannigan there when she went through them before, trying to see if Donny had sold that gun. She didn't think anything of it at the time, of course. And we have four people who say they saw Lannigan there. Nothing to connect him to Donny's gun, though. Although we do have a guy who says he almost bought that gun himself, but couldn't afford it."

"So you can, at minimum, place Lannigan and the murder weapon in the same place at the same time?"

Bax nodded. "Absolutely."

I grinned. "Well, I'd prefer laws that tracked private gun sales better, but I guess I'll take it."

"Yeah," he said. "I don't think a lawyer is going to get Lannigan out of this."

"I have to call Linda," I said. "If she's watching the news online, she's got to be worried sick."

Bax nodded. "She's already loaded in my phone."

I admit that startled me a bit, and I suspect my expression gave that away.

He grinned. "She worries about you, Ed, and she knows you and me get along OK so she calls me now and then, trying to stay up on what's going on. She's a keeper, Ed. Don't fuck it up."

I nodded. "I'll try to keep that in mind."

Bax handed me his phone and walked away, and I moved in the other direction to find a spot away from prying ears.

Linda sounded worried when she answered. "Hi, Scott."

"It's me," I told her.

"Ed! Are you OK?"

"Yes," I said. "Bax let me use his phone. I am nowhere near mine. Brandon Gullick's killer is in custody—well, the ER, but custody if he makes it—and I am OK. Not even going to the hospital this time, but I got hit on the head pretty hard, and they gave me something for pain. I passed their concussion evaluation, anyway."

"Ed, go the hospital and get checked."

"I just got checked, honest. My head hurts, that's all. Everything else is abrasions, contusions, and minor lacerations, as they will no doubt be referred to in Baxter's eventual report."

"Thank God," she said. "You sound OK, I guess."

"You can diagnose me by the sound of my voice?"

"Yes," she said, without hesitation. "I love you."

"I love you, too." I filled her in on some of the other details. I left out the part about the pitchfork. Then I wrapped it up. "I still have to find Donny Blackmon, by the way."

Linda was not happy to hear that.

"Ed, just let the police take it all from here, damn it. You've been shot at enough."

"I understand, but I have to do this."

"Why, exactly? I mean, we pay taxes so we can have cops to go find people, right? And if the officer's killer has been arrested, well, then, can't Donny just come home?"

"Sure," I said. "He could do that. In a perfect world. This is decidedly not a perfect world."

"Just let them do it," she said, in a rather commanding tone. "I am tired of worrying about you."

"Number one," I replied, sounding professorial, "I have as much training, if not more, than most of these guys, right? I was on SWAT, remember."

"Yeah, but you kind of forget training when you get all full of yourself."

I ignored that. "Two, these guys have a lot of work to do, right? They need to tie all the loose ends together, find the evidence to build a case, etcetera. So why divert cops from that? Right? By the way, news does not always move swiftly. Donny probably is keeping his head down, and a lot of cops, and maybe bounty hunters, haven't heard about Lannigan's arrest yet. I think I know where Donny is, by the way. Legwork paid off. But there's still that Blue Fury bounty, lots of cops who don't like Donny. So, if I go find him, I can maybe keep a powder keg from going off."

"Because you're so good at keeping powder kegs from going off!"

"Hey, now."

"Ed, I just want you home. You didn't even tell the cops you think you know where Donny is, did you?"

I gulped. "Well, no."

"I knew it!"

"Remember, some of them want to shoot Donny, maybe. Look, hon, I just want to go up there, find Donny, show him Amy's letter, hand him my phone, and let him call his wife." I pulled the letter from my pocket. It was muddy. "That's it. And then he'll know about his little girl and this will all be over."

Linda gulped. Twice. "Damn it, Ed. You played the little girl card."

"I know. Not fair."

"Just, no more shooting, please?"

"No one is going to shoot me."

"Promise?"

"Promise."

"Be careful. I love you."

"I will. Love you, too."

I ended the call, put away the envelope, and then looked for Bax. I wanted to borrow a gun.

CHAPTER THIRTY-NINE

BAX WAS BUSY talking with local cops and state troopers, so I took a moment to see what I could find out about Mark Babcock while I still had my friend's phone. I found him quickly on Facebook and learned he was a Jesus Conservative who really liked freedoms, guns, dogs, and bluegrass music. He did not much care for Democrats, socialists, liberals, experts, Big Pharma, the Koran, fake news, tramps, cops, and cats.

The parts of all that that gave me immediate concern were the guns and dogs. Those might be a problem.

Once I saw Bax had finished his conversation, I beckoned him toward me and started walking farther out of earshot. The red and blue lights from a half-dozen police vehicles turned the woods into a freak show, an effect enhanced by all the flashlight beams and tall shadows up on the hill. Once Bax caught up to me, I handed him his phone.

"Linda glad to hear you're still kicking?"

"She wants me to come home right now," I said. "And if she finds a cute boring accountant, she might dump me. But my job isn't done." I told him about my plan to go up to the Babcock farm in search of Donny Blackmon.

He grabbed my elbow, stopped me on the road, and stared at me as though I'd told him I planned to poke King Kong in the eye. "Aren't you done with all this solo shit? I mean, you could have gotten killed today. And Donny Blackmon is still a person of interest in all this, whether he had a hand in any killings or not."

"Donny didn't kill anyone," I said.

"Probably," Bax said, looking stern. "Sure. Probably. But just because we know more now than we did yesterday don't mean we know near enough. And Donny is still a gun lover who thinks everyone is on the hunt for him. He is a hair-trigger, Ed. A live wire. We got all kinds of paid, trained officers of the law here, Ed, and they are perfectly capable of going up there to inquire about Donny."

"A guy they hate," I said, "because of his fucking blog. Donny has been a social media sensation in certain circles for months now, Bax. And Babcock's just the type to run in those circles. Check out his Facebook. If a bunch of cops go up to that farm, God knows what they'll run into. We don't want a bunch of people shooting at one another when it is completely avoidable, do we?"

"They can handle the situation," he answered.

I looked at the cops on the road and the shadows in the trees. "They don't have to handle it. Look, Donny probably has flown the coop already. He knows he almost got caught at the festival, but he doesn't know I was there mostly playing on a hunch. As far as he knows, someone actually did some real detective work and connected him to Babcock, and that's why I was there. So I doubt he's even there, but that's where the new trail starts. So let me go up there, talk to Babcock, see if I can pick up the scent. I'm hoping once all the news about Lannigan's arrest breaks, these guys might actually believe it, and Donny will come out of hiding. That might take a while, though. These are not people who trust the media or government or get vaccinated and wear masks and all that."

Bax stared at me.

"I have to do this," I told him.

"I don't get it," he said. "Why?"

I figured the only way I could get Bax to trust me was for me to trust him.

"Donny's little girl has cancer," I whispered. "That is top secret, by the way. Amy does not want that to become the next big news cycle. Amy hired me to find her husband, just to tell him that." I pulled the envelope out of my pocket. "This is a letter she wrote to Donny. I'm supposed to get it to him. Amy can't get hold of him any better than anyone else. She doesn't want the whole universe to know about her family's troubles because they're not whiners, and she figures the media and cops will just use that news to draw Donny out. Hell, the Blackmons hate the press as much as they hate the government and the cops."

Bax lowered his eyes and stared at the dark road. "I know how she is," he said.

"Bax, that little girl looked me in the eyes and said, 'Go find Daddy.' I have to do that. Donny might go home, eventually, if it ever really does sink in that he's off the hook for the Gullick murder, but how long is that going to take? Days? Weeks? Months? Meanwhile, his girl needs a daddy right now. Who knows how much time she's got?"

"Yeah," he said. He was choking up a bit. Detective Scott Baxter was more good, caring human than hardened cop.

I decided this was a sign I should press my luck. "I really don't think we need a bunch of cops descending on the Babcock farm, do you? I mean, Donny's probably not there, and he's more of a witness now than a suspect, right?"

He nodded. "I reckon." Then he paused to think. "OK," he said, finally. "I will keep my mouth shut for now. But you call me. I want to know what you know before you even know it, got me?"

I nodded. "Amen. Absolutely. You'll get sick of my calls, they'll be so frequent. You'll block my number, drop me on Facebook, all that, I'll be updating you so much."

"Fine. I'll give you a ride to your truck."

I decided against asking him to lend me a gun. I thought that might change his mind.

As we opened the doors to Bax's Jeep, a large man in a Pike County Sheriff's Office uniform approached. "Detective Baxter?"

"Major Keyes," Bax said. "Something new? Ed, this is Major Alan Keyes."

Major Keyes was not quite my height, but he was broad of shoulder, and his biceps were pushing the limits of his uniform sleeves. His eyes were stony gray, and he had a bright blond mustache that looked like it would not wobble in a tornado. "Well, sir, I just wanted to ask you, where the hell are you going?"

"He's taking me to my truck, Major."

Keyes looked at me. "And I am wondering why that's even being considered, since I have about six million questions I need to ask you, Runyon."

"I provided full statements to your men, sir."

"And now I want you to talk to me. You drove a pitchfork through a man in my county," he said. He was not going to be as malleable as Baxter. I could tell.

"In self-defense," I said.

"So you tell us." The major spat some tobacco on the pavement. "You were involved in that fracas in Waverly, too. It's all just an awful lot of stuff that I am keen to hear about."

Baxter intervened. "Major Keyes, I've worked with Ed, known him several years, and I'm sure he's telling the truth."

Keyes stepped closer to Baxter. "And I've known you, Detective, for what? About three hours?"

The lawmen stared at one another. I wondered if Major Keyes ever blinked.

"What's the goddamned hurry, anyway?" Keyes' eyes narrowed as he asked. He was a dog on a scent.

I jumped in. "Well, sir, I am a private investigator visiting in Pike County and working on a case, and I want to get back to it."

"What case is that?"

"Missing person," I said.

"Donny Blackmon," he said. "You're looking for Donny Blackmon."

"Yes."

"I want to know why, exactly."

I inhaled sharply. "I am not at liberty to discuss my client's business, sir."

"A man with a pitchfork!" I thought for a moment he was going to throw his broad-brimmed hat on the road and stomp on it. "I have a man with a pitchfork in his goddamned chest, and you say you put it there. I want to ask you a lot of questions, Runyon, and I want to ask every one of them about twenty times!"

"I made an agreement with my client," I told him. "I am not inclined to share my client's personal business."

"Now you wait a goddamned minute, Runyon." His eyes looked more like stone than they had before. Sharper, too, like they could dissect me.

"Sir," Baxter said. "You've gone over what Ed told your men?"

"Yes, of course!"

"Have you talked to your men at the barn scene?"

"Next on my list."

Baxter nodded. "How about this. You talk to them, see if the evidence at the scene meshes with Ed's testimony, while we wait here. You can decide whether you need to talk to Ed now, or if it can wait, of course. I am sure Ed will be cooperative."

Keyes started pacing. He stopped after six turns and looked right at me. "Do you know where Donny Blackmon is?"

"I do not," I said.

His "don't bullshit me" face was one of the best I've ever seen. "You sure about that?"

"Yes."

"But you have a lead." That was not a question.

"I have a very thin, slender, tenuous lead, made out of fog and hopes, that might possibly put me back on the trail. But, remember, Lannigan has pretty much confessed to the murder of Officer Brandon Gullick."

"So you say," Keyes said. "He didn't talk much to our people when they dragged him out of the woods. He was kind of quiet and pale by then."

"I'm sure the evidence at the barn will mesh with Ed's testimony," Baxter said.

"Wait here." The major stomped off and barked into a walkie-talkie.

"I hope the evidence at the scene meshes with your testimony," Bax said.

"It will."

We stood there by Bax's Jeep, awaiting the major's return. When he came back, he got right to business.

"We have fresh tracks all over, showing three men running and/or sidestepping around the barn. We have tire tracks that ought to match that vehicle, which is registered to the guy with the pitchfork." He pointed at Jerry Spence's Toyota. "And that vehicle has blood in the back seat, consistent with your account of Lannigan getting shot. We haven't confirmed it's his blood, of course. Not yet."

Keyes came closer and almost put his mustache in my face. "I don't like any of this, Runyon."

"Neither do I," I said. "I'd rather be off having a beer and listening to banjos."

"What you are going to do," he said, "is come with me to the SO right now. I am going to ask you a lot of things, Runyon, while my people do their homework on you. After that, I'll decide whether to hold you or let you go."

"Fair enough," I said.

CHAPTER FORTY

MAJOR KEYES STARED at me for an hour, asking the same questions in different ways to see if I contradicted myself. He was good at it, too, and by the end I was awfully goddamned glad I was telling the truth.

He decided I was being honest, apparently. "Runyon, I'm not going to hold you. If you have a line on Donny Blackmon, I'd like to think you'd share that with your friend Baxter, but it's not my case, and I'll let you work that out with him."

"Thanks, Major."

"You will, of course, be available to my men when they have follow-up questions for you, and you will let us know where you are staying."

"Of course."

He let out a big gush of air. "I hope you find Blackmon," he said. "Someone's going to kill him if they get the chance." He paused for a long time, shaking his head. "Believe it or not, I don't think he killed that officer. I was convinced, but, well, not now."

"Thank you, Major."

Bax took me to my truck. "I thought he'd decide to hold you," he said.

"Maybe next time."

After I was reunited with my truck and phone, I weighed whether to wait until morning before going up to the Babcock farm. I decided to press onward. The longer I waited, the colder Donny's new trail would get.

I doused myself as best I could with a water bottle and grabbed my last clean T-shirt out of my bag, a gray three-quarter sleeve emblazoned with the Ohio State "Block O" logo. Then I aimed the Ford for the Babcock farm.

It was easier to find in the dark than I thought it would be because the makeshift signs directing people to the Mud Run Bluegrass Festival had not yet been taken down. I turned up the narrow gravel road. I was unable to see much of anything other than what my headlights showed, because tall trees crowded the road on both sides. Several of those trees bore "No Trespassing" signs, which I ignored.

Any of those trees could be hiding gunmen, ready for anyone who might come looking for Donny Blackmon.

I kept going anyway.

I passed by the turnoff that led to the festival grounds and kept heading toward the house. The road started going uphill, and the trees seemed thicker. I could tell there was a moon up there somewhere, though, because a little soft light danced around the treetops.

Something moved on the road ahead, and I braked. I ducked, too, because I was honestly nowhere near as calm about this little mission as I'd tried to sound when I talked to Bax.

No gun roared out, and my windshield did not shatter. When I looked up, I was staring at a doe. She stared back. I turned off my headlights, and she eventually wandered off into the woods.

I waited to see if there were any others, but there weren't. An owl hooted somewhere. "Who cooks for you?" That's how naturalists describe the call.

Linda. Linda cooks for me. I hoped she'd get to keep doing that. And I wanted to make her a pot of chili, too. Lots of pots of chili.

I lit up the road again and moved on. My truck handled the incline pretty well, but I imagined the average car would not have.

The road leveled off into a clearing, and I could see the house. A large log cabin ranch with a wraparound porch and lots of windows, most with light spilling out of them. I rolled slowly across the clearing until I was close enough to the house to shout and hope someone inside would hear me. Then I stopped the truck and got out.

In the clearing now, I could see stars again. It was a lovely night.

I heard an awful lot of clicks around me, the kind of clicks you hear when someone pulls back on a gun hammer or pumps a new round into a shotgun. Too many clicks to count.

I figured I must have driven over an alarm trigger somewhere on the road or been seen by a camera or two mounted in the trees.

I raised my hands, very slowly.

"You're trespassing. Who the hell are you?" A cigarette lighter flared and illuminated the bushy face of Mark Babcock, about twenty feet away. He puffed on a cigar and wasn't even looking at me. Why should he? I was surrounded by loaded guns.

"My name is Ed Runyon," I said, trying to sound relaxed. "Donny Blackmon's wife hired me to find her husband, and I think you might know where he is."

Something sniffed at my knee. I looked down and saw a werewolf. The black dog had to lean his head down to smell at my knee. His shoulder was considerably higher than my knee.

"That's Ace," Babcock said. "He's got your scent now, just in case you were thinking to run and hide."

"I didn't come up for trouble," I said, trying to ignore the dog who was now in front of me, large white teeth distractingly close to my crotch.

"That's good to hear." Babcock looked up. The cigar glow didn't quite reveal all the details, so he looked even more like a gorilla in a cowboy hat than he did the first time I saw him. And he seemed taller, too. I wondered if he was standing on something, or if he was really that big.

"I don't know anything about a guy named Blackmon," he said. "And you're still trespassing."

"I saw him here last night, at the festival," I said.

Babcock shrugged. "A lot of people came to the festival," he said. "The smart ones left when it was over. You're still here and no longer a guest. So, you are a trespasser, and if you haven't noticed, you are surrounded by guns. And Ace." Babcock whistled sharply, and Ace loped to his side.

"I did notice that," I replied. "If they all shoot at once, they are likely to hurt each other as much as they hurt me."

Babcock laughed. "Hell. Rick, if I give the go-ahead, you be the one to shoot him."

"Nice!" I assumed that was Rick. He sounded like he'd just won the lottery. He was behind me, too.

"The rest of you hold off a bit so you don't kill one another," Babcock continued. "Now, what did you say your name was, mister?"

"Ed Runyon."

"Mr. Runyon, I want you to get in your truck and drive away. No one here knows this guy you are looking for, and no one here wants to get involved in whatever this is. So just get off my property, nice and peaceful. Do anything else, and nice and peaceful ain't going to happen."

"Mr. Babcock," I said, stepping slowly toward my truck and keeping my hands high, "Donny is in the clear. The police caught the guy who killed that cop in Ambletown. They have him in custody, and they have enough evidence to convict. You'll see it on the news. Tell Donny it's true. Tell Donny to call his wife."

"I don't know what you are talking about," he said.

"Please, sir, just tell Donny to call his wife. She has things she needs to tell him."

His poker face broke, but only for a moment. "Just get in the truck and drive away, real slow."

I did a slow spin, hoping to maybe get a glimpse of Donny. It was too dark to really tell, but all four of the guys surrounding me seemed to be too big. Two had shotguns, the others had pistols.

When I was facing Babcock again, I said, "Can I leave one of my cards with you? If you decide you remember something, you can call me?"

His cigar flared. Then he exhaled slowly and said, "Rick."

Babcock touched the dog's head. Ace stared at me and growled.

I got in the truck. Once the engine started, I grabbed one of my cards from the console and tossed it outside on the ground. "In case you remember something," I said. "But please, just tell Donny to call his wife. He needs to. Soon."

I drove away.

CHAPTER FORTY-ONE

ONCE I WAS off the Babcock property and my heart rate was at something less than the tempo of "Foggy Mountain Breakdown," I called Bax.

For once, he skipped the "I'm so happy to hear from you" routine. "Well?"

"Hi, Bax, I'm fine. Family doing well?"

"Shut up and tell me what happened."

I sighed. "I was greeted with accusations of trespassing and a lot of loaded guns, and Mr. Babcock and his assembled guests disavowed any notion of knowing one Donny Blackmon."

"Could have guessed," he said.

"I know, but I had to look, and hey, no one shot at me this time. They have a werewolf, though."

Bax ignored that. "Any clues as to whether Donny is there?"

"None," I told him. "Too dark to see much, and I never made it inside the house. But they were on a hair-trigger, though. I mean, guns out as soon as I got out of the truck. I was surrounded. Maybe they were all just nervous about the cops and helicopters combing the area, maybe they're hiding tons of cocaine on the premises, or maybe Donny Blackmon is there and they are protecting him.

Whatever it is, I'm sure all the choppers and cops in the area all day had them spooked."

"You had a guy tell you he sent Donny to Babcock for work, right? And he saw them together?"

"Yeah," I said. "I mean, he was going off my description so there is no absolute certainty, but, yeah."

Bax thought for a moment. "We can get a warrant and go search, might find Donny, or evidence that tells us where he went."

"No," I told him. "Don't do that. It'll just stir those guys up. They have someone named Rick who sounds like he just can't wait to shoot someone. And don't forget the werewolf."

"Werewolf?"

"Well, big dog. Anyway, I say we let the news drop, maybe we'll get lucky and Donny will call his wife."

"I guess you are right," he said. "No reason to charge hard, I guess. It'd be like painting a barn you already knocked down."

"Bax," I said, "I think that metaphor actually works."

"What's a metaphor?"

"Doesn't matter. How's Lannigan?"

"Lost a good bit of blood, but nothing vital was hit. He's probably going to make it, doctors say."

"Thanks."

I ended the call and punched up Amy Blackmon's number.

"Hello, Mr. Runyon." She sounded nervous.

"Hi, Amy. I'm calling to update you. I got very, very close to Donny but he slipped away. He's found some friends who are helping him. But the good news is the police have found out who killed Officer Gullick. It wasn't Donny. The killer is in custody."

She was silent for a moment. Then it seemed she was mumbling a prayer. Finally, she spoke. "This isn't some kind of trick? The cops would love to put one over on Donny. They hate him."

"No, it's not a trick. I won't lie to you, Amy. I know what you and Cassie are going through. I've seen Officer Gullick's killer myself. I know he did it. He's bad hurt, in the hospital, but sounds like he'll pull through and then he'll face trial. Donny is in the clear. Watch the news—you'll see it all."

"I'll watch." She still sounded dubious.

"I honestly expect Donny to call you soon," I said. "I've spoken with people who helped him—they deny knowing him, of course, but I think they're lying to me to protect him—anyway, I didn't tell them anything about your family situation, but I did tell them Donny needs to call you. I don't know if they can contact Donny or not, but if they can, I think they'll tell him you hired me to look for him. So he may call."

"God, I hope so."

"How is Cassie?"

"Bravest little girl on Earth," Amy said. Then she gulped. "Braver than me."

"You're both brave," I said. "I have some other leads I'm going to follow up. I'll keep looking until Donny calls you."

"Thank you."

My next call was to Linda. I could tell she'd been worried. "Are you OK?"

"I am fine. Worn out, smelly, need a shower and fresh clothes. Hungry as hell. And I've earned a beer or two. Still haven't found Donny, though." I filled her in on the latest details.

"He's got to call her now, though, right? I mean, he's innocent. Reporters on Twitter are saying there's been a break in the case, someone is in custody . . ."

"The first thing Amy said when I told her Donny was in the clear was that it might be a trap. I think she half believes me, but only half. And don't forget Blue Fury. Those guys say they'll pay big bucks for Donny's head on a platter. Have they backed off yet?"

"I don't know. I block people who talk about that shit on Twitter and Facebook, you know that. Jesus," Linda said. "This world where nobody trusts anybody is getting really old. Are you coming home now?"

"I'm going to clean up and get some sleep. And I'm going to ask around tomorrow. My guess is that Donny bolted as soon as he could after I found him. Babcock or one of his guys probably gave Donny a ride somewhere and dropped him off. He could be a hundred miles away or more. I'm basically just going to see if I can pick up the trail and keep looking until Donny hears about the Lannigan arrest and calls his wife."

"So no shooting or chasing or anything like that?"

"Should be OK from here on out," I said.

"OK. I love you."

"Love you, too."

CHAPTER FORTY-TWO

My buzzing phone awoke me.

I answered, because I don't ignore unknown numbers when I am working a case. "Runyon."

"Everything I'm about to tell you is just hypothetical." The caller did not identify himself, but he sounded like a gorilla in a cowboy hat, smoking a cigar. "I do not want to be dragged into any of this shit, cops getting killed, bounty hunters, all that."

"Understood," I said. I sat up, more alert than usual after being awake for less than a minute. I looked around the hotel room for my Mountain Dew bottle and wished the coffee was already made.

"After that fugitive almost got nabbed at the bluegrass festival, it's possible he was very scared," the man said. "He had been eluding everyone for months, you see, but he probably thought he'd fucked that up just to play some music."

"Hypothetically," I said.

"Right. Anyway, a guy like that might turn to a friend, even in the middle of the night, and get the hell out of there, you know what I mean?"

"Sure. That's what I'd do, I think. Any idea where a friend might take this fugitive, theoretically?"

"Well, it is conceivable in my mind that this friend might have driven the fugitive to Columbus, at the fugitive's direction," he said. "I'd guess anyone in that much trouble would turn to a church."

"That sounds reasonable, Mister—"

"Say my name and I hang up," he said.

"Of course. Sorry. Would you, whoever you are and I officially have no goddamned idea who you are, have any idea what church in Columbus our hypothetical fugitive might have sought out?"

I heard an exhalation and imagined a plume of cigar smoke swirling around a bearded face under the brim of a cowboy hat. "Well, if I was to reflect on matters for a while and try to come up with the best possible answer to that question, I might come up with God's Fellowship Church, east side, not far from downtown."

"And, theoretically speaking, of course, that is where the fugitive asked his hypothetical friend to take him?"

"That would be my uninformed analysis of the facts as I know them," he said, "being someone who does not really know anything about any of this, mind you."

"Do you think the fugitive is still there?"

"No idea," he answered. "The friend never even saw him go into the church, in this hypothetical situation."

"Can we stop saying hypothetical and theoretical?" I stood up and started pacing. "I mean, it's understood, all of this is just two guys playing guessing games, right?"

"Sure," he said.

"Do you have a number for this fugitive?"

"No."

"Do you have a name and a number for anyone at this church?"

"No."

"Is there anything like a drop box, a place where friends and allies can leave this fugitive a message?"

"No. The fugitive is not that stupid." He paused. "Theoretically."

"Do you have any other good guesses or intuitions that might help me find this fugitive?"

"I believe all of my hypothetical insights have been proffered," he said. That was followed by another long, calm exhalation.

"Thank you for sharing your highly speculative notions with me."

"I want to emphasize this point," he said. "I do not want to be dragged into any of this shit. I definitely would not want to be the man who dragged me into this shit. That man would be very, very sorry."

"I have absolutely no doubt," I told him. I wasn't kidding. The calm sense of menace in Mark Babcock's voice was quite chilling, and I already knew how he greeted unwanted guests. "I have to ask, sir. Why did you decide to call me?"

He paused before answering. "I watched the news this morning," he said. "All the shit you told some guys, theoretically, of course, came to pass. The cop charged with killing that other cop, I mean. And from what I hear on the grapevine, you went unarmed into a place you probably didn't want to go and probably should not have gone, and all you asked was that a man call his wife. If what I hear is true, because let me stress that I was not there and did not tell anyone he could shoot you if you moved, so all this is only shit I heard, but if it is true, that took some guts."

"Well, if you ever run into those guys, tell Rick thanks for not shooting me. And scratch Ace behind the ears. I appreciate all this speculative advice, sir."

"Don't mention it," he said. "And I fucking mean that literally."

I hung up, got some coffee going, and grabbed a quick shower. As I cleaned up, I thought about a movie called *The 13th Warrior*, which features a bunch of Norsemen pitted against some head-hunting cannibals. It might seem weird that I thought of that, but a line from the movie ran through my head. The Norse leader had told an elderly king that luck will often save a man, if his courage holds up, or words to that effect. I had not felt particularly brave with all of those guns pointed at me and a big dog sniffing at my nether regions, but it apparently had paid off. If you just keep going, sometimes you get there.

I dressed in clean clothes purchased the previous evening and grabbed my coffee.

On the way to the lobby, I called the Pike County Sheriff's Office.

"Ed Runyon," I said. "Please tell Major Keyes I am going to church in Columbus. I can be reached at this number."

I ended the call before anyone got a chance to ask for further explanation.

CHAPTER FORTY-THREE

ABOUT TWO HOURS later, I was pulling into the lot of a mostly dilapidated storefront that now was serving as a mostly dilapidated church, on a side street off East Long Street farther from downtown Columbus than I'd expected from Mark Babcock's description. Some windows were still boarded up, but someone had used spray paint and some nice calligraphy to place a sign over the door. It said: GOD'S FELLOWSHIP CHURCH.

No one seemed to be around.

I had done some googling earlier and found the church's number, but I had not called. I didn't want to take any chance at all of spooking Donny Blackmon if he was still here. I decided a direct approach would be best, or at least would look the least suspicious to anyone watching from inside, so I got out of the truck and walked up to the door.

I knocked. No answer.

I knocked again. Same result.

I started walking clockwise around the building. Not all of the windows were boarded, so I peeked inside. I saw nothing but mismatched pews, possibly collected from other churches, and a simple pulpit in front of a simple, rugged cross. Hymnals and Bibles dotted the pews. Stained glass windows, framed in wood, leaned against a wall awaiting installation.

I heard a door slam behind the building and moved toward the sound. I entered an alley between the church and a tall wooden fence. A screen door at the back of the church was swinging on its hinges.

Beyond all that, I saw a person vanish over the top of the fence. I saw little, but I saw enough—the man was bald, with tattoos on his scalp. Maybe it was Donny Blackmon, maybe it wasn't, but I was going to find out.

I took off at a dead run and leapt, grabbing the top of the fence. I swung up a leg, paused at the top to make sure I wasn't about to leap into a pile of glass or scrap metal—and the top of the fence next to me splintered in the wake of a loud, sharp crack.

Donny had a gun.

I dropped and dove for cover behind a child's sandbox, while a man at the back door of a home yelled "Jesus" and ran back inside.

Donny was running down a driveway between two homes. He turned right at the sidewalk and vanished.

"Donny!" I took off after him.

By the time I got to the street, Donny was disappearing again, this time by running up a driveway. A young woman pushing a stroller across the street glanced my way. I shouted a warning. "Active shooter! Get out of here! Take cover!" I didn't know a stroller could move so fast.

I followed Donny and did not get shot. When I had him in sight again, he was heading up another alley toward East Long Street. I kept going in his wake.

He made a few more turns, but I was able to keep my eyes on him. Soon, he was dodging traffic on Long Street and headed toward an ugly, weed-pierced asphalt parking lot. He was too busy not getting hit by cars to take a good shot at me, so I took the opportunity to close the distance.

He was across by the time I reached the road. I looked both ways at a fast run, which is not the recommended way to do it, and managed to get to the opposite side in one piece. But I'd lost sight of Donny because I'd had to pay attention to an SUV.

Donny found me before I found him. I heard the shot, but felt nothing, and assumed I'd not been hit. But the sound directed my eyes, and I saw Donny Blackmon kneeling on black, cracked pavement, a handgun aimed right at me and his gaze directed right along the sights.

I was pretty sure Donny, gun blogger that he was, would not miss me if he tried again, so I dropped and rolled.

He missed me a third time, and got up and ran. I reckoned he'd figured out by now that I was unarmed. My weapon, of course, was in an evidence room in Pike County.

I rose and did a quick spin to see if any innocent bystanders had been hit. No one was around except the people driving down Long Street, and they seemed oblivious. I resumed my pursuit.

Donny disappeared behind some kind of fast-food chicken joint. I rounded the corner behind him. He whipped around, fired a wild shot that had no goddamned chance of hitting an intended target, and ran again.

This was going to get someone killed. Probably me.

I stopped running, and bellowed as loud as I could. "Cassie's sick!"

He kept running.

"Your daughter is very sick, Donny!"

He stopped.

He turned.

He aimed.

I dropped to my knees, hands in the air. He walked slowly toward me. He kept glancing from side to side, probably expecting SWAT or the CIA or the Spanish Inquisition to emerge from neighboring properties to take him in or gun him down.

I was panting hard, but I got the words out. "I am unarmed. I am not a cop, not a bounty hunter. Your wife hired me to find you and ask you to call her. Cassie is very ill. She needs you."

Being surrounded by Mark Babcock's good ol' boys with guns was nowhere near as intimidating as looking at Donny Blackmon with his gun aimed at my head. He was breathing hard, his eyes were wild, and he looked very, very confused.

"Just call her," I said. Talking was a bit easier as my breath returned to normal. "You're in the clear for the cop's murder, Donny. We found the guy who did it. He's in custody. We know you didn't do it."

He looked more confused than he did before, and his hands were moving around in a way that told me they were sweating. His aim was shaky, and I started to fear he was going to drill a hole in my brain by accident.

"I have a letter from your wife," I said. "In my pocket. I am not going to reach for it. I am going to keep my hands high where you can see them. But you can have the letter. She said you would know it's from her."

He shook his head, violently. "No fucking way. I am not getting any closer."

"Shit, Donny. OK. Just borrow a phone," I said. "Check the news. Call Amy. She'll tell you. Just call Amy."

Donny didn't say a word. He just looked at me, gun trained on my face, shaking like he was in a meat freezer.

I was shaking, too. I'd had guns pointed my way, of course. I'd even been shot at a few times. Hell, since becoming a private investigator, I was even getting used to it. Just an occupational haz-ard. Accountants get headaches from staring at a screen, store clerks get headaches from dealing with assholes all day, I get shot at. No big deal.

But my mind could not dredge up a memory of ever staring at a gun for that long, wondering if the guy with his finger on the trigger was going to squeeze it or not. It took forever. I had plenty of time to wonder what hot lead would feel like tunneling through my gray matter. Would I hear the shot, or would the bullet already be in my head by the time sound reached my ears and tripped all the pieces in my auditory canal?

I did not want to find out. But there was not a goddamned thing I could do about it.

All I could do was stare at him and try to impose my will on him. *Believe me*, I silently commanded.

Not that I thought it would do a damned bit of good. I was well aware of how far down the "cops are evil" rabbit hole Donny Black-mon had plunged. I'd seen all the Facebook conversations—if you can call them that—between people who wanted us all to wear masks and get the shots and those who were convinced COVID-19 was just a government plot to steal our freedoms. Believing things said by people who are on the other side of everything does not come naturally to the human species.

I've been told I have an honest face. I've also been told I look a little like the actor who played the Joker in *The Dark Knight*, and that dude was one untrustworthy motherfucker. I had no idea whether Donny had seen that movie or not, but he probably had. Almost everyone had.

I was pretty certain Donny Blackmon was going to shoot me.

And then he didn't.

Instead, he turned and ran.

I fell forward, in a heap, and almost broke my nose. Every limb felt useless, and air came in big, horrible-sounding gasps. I think it took me at least a minute to decide that, yes, I was going to live another day and, hmm, maybe I should call someone out there in the world and let them know what the hell was going on.

CHAPTER FORTY-FOUR

JIM LANNIGAN DID survive his blood loss. They had him in the Mifflin County Jail, awaiting trial. He'd found a good lawyer, a woman named Casey Dettorre who'd been defending cases in Mifflin County for ten years and had an amazing track record. Her client was not making her job easy, though. I had not been there as Detective Baxter and other deputies had interviewed him, but Bax was telling me all about it after I offered to buy him lunch at Tuck's. It had been three weeks since Donny Blackmon had aimed a gun at my face, and I wanted to know more about the Gullick murder than I was getting from the news accounts.

"Damnedest thing, Ed," Bax said after swallowing a bite of cheeseburger. "The man won't just shut up. Like a leaky faucet full of poop, just runs on and on and on."

Rather than ask why anyone would have a faucet that pours poop, I just asked about Lannigan. "So, he confessed to everything?"

Bax nodded, and finished up his fries. He glanced up at one of the buck heads mounted across the room, an eight-pointer. "Shot one like that once, when I was sixteen." Then he got back on topic. "Yeah, Lannigan told it all. Every damned thing. He says his life is over. Tells everyone, his jailers, the guy in the next cell, the ceiling at night when he's supposed to be asleep. His lawyer's got to be weeping at night, too."

I shook my head in disbelief. "Wish all crooks made life this easy."

"He's on constant suicide watch," Bax added. "Sad. I can't believe a cop would do what he did. But he just went nuts after he found out about Gullick and his wife. Just batshit bonkers."

Tuck interrupted us to deliver another round of beers, IPA for me and a lager for Bax. The tray held a third glass, full of something dark as cola but with a brown foam on top. "Mind if I join you, gentlemen?" Tuck sat down. "I want to hear the details, too. This world doesn't make too much sense anymore. I'm just trying to understand, you know?"

I looked at Bax, who raised his eyebrows and said, "Sure. But keep quiet about it."

"Of course," Tuck replied, raising his glass.

I pointed at Tuck's drink. "Something from Ireland, I suppose?"

"Nope. Columbus. A Russian imperial stout called Filthy McNasty, from North High Brewing Company," he said. "The name sounded like it would pair well with the conversational topic, right?" He seemed a little on edge, despite having a beer and sitting down with friends. Tuck is, perhaps, the most peaceful person I know. As sweet as Linda is, I could envision her getting angry and clawing some asshole's face more easily than I could see Tuck doing the same. The idea of murder rattles him.

Bax pointed at Tuck's glass. "Russian imperial what?"

"Don't get him started on beer," I implored. "We'll be on that subject all day. Get back to Lannigan. Did he think his plan was going to work?"

Bax shrugged. "He wasn't really thinking at all, I guess. I mean, not proper. He was, is, really messed up. I think he loves his wife as much as he hates her."

"So what was his plan, then?" Tuck was leaning closer to Bax.

"He waited for Brandon to go on his morning run," the detective said. "Daily thing, everyone knows it. Anyway, Lannigan set an ambush, caught Brandon from behind, and shoved chloroform into his face. Then he hustled him into a vehicle and drove him to Donny's barn, using the back way from Dream Road. He figured to dump the body there and let us all blame Donny Blackmon."

Tuck winced. "That's cold. How was he going to explain the cop being on Donny's property, though?"

I laughed. "Lannigan wasn't worried about that at all. He was going to just let Donny try to explain it. Anything Donny said was going to sound like a fairy tale, of course. I mean, the best he might come up with would be to say he didn't know how a dead cop ended up on his farm. Guys who kill people say they don't know how their DNA got smeared all over a corpse all the time. Prosecutors and juries kind of just ignore that shit."

Tuck thought about that. "Makes sense, I guess. And he was going to let Donny explain the gun, too? The one Lannigan bought at the gun show?"

I shook my head. "That seems the most amateur-hour thing of all, to me," I said. "Leaving Donny's gun there. I mean, no way would a killer do that. Has Lannigan never investigated a homicide?"

Bax put his glass on the table. "That," he said, "was an accident. Lannigan either fucked up the chloroform or Gullick had one hell of a constitution, but anyway, once he got his victim to the barn, Gullick put up a fight. Fists, kicks, whole works. Lannigan whacked him with a board while they fought over the gun. Must have been a scene, man, like you and your pitchfork, Ed."

"One does what one must do," I said. "Carry on."

"Well, Lannigan got separated from Gullick and finally . . ." Bax paused, and gulped. "He did what he was there to do, but it all took him a lot longer than he'd planned. He heard a shout and turns and, boom, there's Donny."

"Surprise," Tuck said.

Bax continued. "Donny throws a couple of rocks at him, or something, maybe, hell, who knows what he threw, but Jim ducks and loses the gun in the grass."

"Well, now," I said. "That makes more sense."

"Yeah," Bax said with a nod. "His plan had to have been to toss it into Wild Creek off Dream Road. He figured we'd match the bullet to the type of gun, the Sig Sauer, and that we'd figure out eventually that a Sig that had been featured on Donny's blog was missing. Whether we'd have dragged the creek or not, he couldn't control, of course, although I suppose he could have just suggested it during the investigation, right? Hey, guys, maybe drag the creek, see if the murder weapon was discarded? Something like that."

Tuck shook his head, slowly. "Man, this is all diabolical."

"Yeah," Bax said. "Anyway, so Donny panics and runs, Lannigan panics and can't find the gun, so he gets the hell out of there, and, well, there you have it."

I pointed at Bax. "I'll bet you ten dollars Lannigan showed up at the crime scene very soon after Amy found Brandon's body."

"He did," Bax said. "Absolutely. One of the first on the scene, in fact. Just happened to be in the area when the call came in, he said. Because he had to be, of course."

Tuck looked confused. "Why?"

Bax and I answered him in unison. "Tire tracks."

Tuck smacked his forehead. "His car tracks were on the scene from when he took Brandon up there."

"Maybe, maybe not." Bax shrugged. "Dirt road, sure, you get tracks, so he'd counted on that. And it rained a while that morning, after the killing, but he couldn't count on that obliterating anything.

So he'd planned all along to get there fast once the body was reported, and he came from the Dream Road direction. So if investigators found Lannigan's tracks there, they'd just think it happened when he came on the scene."

"Yep," I said.

Tuck whispered. "Diabolical. To think that hard about things, just to kill a man, I mean, how long had this anger been rolling around in his head? So much planning, pinning it on another man. I can't understand it, man. I just can't."

"It happens," I said. "Sad, but it happens." This pretty much summed up all of my wisdom on the subject, despite a career in law enforcement.

Bax picked up his vibrating phone and glanced at the screen. "Shit, guys. I gotta go. What do I owe you, Tuck?"

Tuck started to toss out a number, but I stopped him. "I got this, Bax. And I'll even pay off some of my tab."

"Really?" Bax said, standing up. "Thanks, Ed, I appreciate it. I'll get the next one."

I reached into my wallet and pulled out a fifty. "Keep the change," I said. "Thanks for all the free beers and burgers."

Tuck plucked the nice clean bill from my fingers. "We'll call it even. I never really kept a tab."

I walked out into the sunshine and called Linda as I crossed the street to my truck.

"Hey there," she said. "Nice lunch?"

"Yeah, Bax was in a talkative mood. I'll tell you about it later."

"OK. Are you headed home? Pick up milk if you can."

"I'll get some, but it will be a little later. I've got to head to the Blackmon farm."

She paused. "Nervous?"

"Just a little. But it'll be fine. I know it will."

"Kisses when you get home," she said.

I got in the truck, popped a CD I'd purchased at the Mud Run Bluegrass Festival into the player, and revved up the engine. Banjo breakdowns make me push the speed limit a bit.

CHAPTER FORTY-FIVE

As I DREW closer to the Blackmon home, I watched the trees and barns.

The Blue Fury people, whoever the hell they were, had gone silent as far as any bounty on Donny's head, but a lot of people still speculated about them online. And Donny was still hero to some, villain to others, and there was always a chance that someone out there still thought they could make a bundle by killing Donny Blackmon.

People online brought up Blue Fury every time a police officer was killed in the line of duty, too. Would the mystery organization put up a reward for the killer's death? Many believed they would. I remain convinced the internet was not humanity's greatest idea. Prove me wrong.

I figured this Blue Fury shit would never go away, but I also knew law enforcement, including the FBI, was trying to track down the originators. I hoped they'd be caught. The last thing this country needs is people encouraging the masses to take up their guns and hunt other people.

Anyway, the Blue Fury assholes had riled up a lot of people, so I watched for ambushes behind every tree and barn as I got closer to the Blackmon farm. I was getting somewhat tired of being in gunsights.

Speaking of which, I had not seen Donny Blackmon since the day he'd aimed his gun at my face. I had no idea what kind of greeting I'd get from him. I prepared myself to see another gun, because that seems to be how my luck rolls.

I shut off the music, parked the truck next to a raised flower bed, and strolled up to the house.

Amy answered the door. "Ed! Come on in. Donny's in the kitchen, making sandwiches with Cassie. Want one?" Deep worries still showed on her face, despite her warm welcome, but she had brightened up some since she'd hired me.

"No, but thanks," I said. "I wanted to come out here because I have something for you."

"Oh, you've done plenty," she said, and I could tell she meant it. "You should have let me pay you. I still intend to, when we can. Don't fret about that."

"No," I said. "We're good. Let me explain."

Before I could do that, though, Cassie came running out of the kitchen, waving a peanut butter sandwich. I could tell it was peanut butter because it was spread so thick it was oozing out from between the bread slices. "Mr. Runyon! Hello, Mr. Runyon!" She was all bright eyes and big smile. You'd never know this kid had cancer, judging by her behavior at the moment. She wrapped me in a big warm hug, accidentally dropping her sandwich on my shoes. "Thank you, Mr. Runyon!"

I suppressed the urge to cry. I had not seen this girl in a while. I'd avoided the Blackmon home since learning Donny had come out of hiding, and now I felt guilty about that. If Cassie could be tough, why couldn't I?

Jesus.

"Hi, Cassie," I said. "It's always nice to see you."

As we stood there surrounded by all the guns encased for display on the wall, Donny appeared at the kitchen entrance. His hair was growing back, and he'd put on a little weight. I could not tell from his eyes whether he wanted to shoot me.

"I have something for you all," I said, after Cassie had disentangled herself from me. She picked up her sandwich.

"Don't eat that, honey," Amy said. "I'll make you another one. What do you have for us, Ed?" Cassie ran off to the kitchen to throw away her soiled sandwich.

I suppressed a grin. "Would she really have eaten that?"

"Who knows," Amy said. "Kids."

I took an envelope from my back pocket. "There were various police groups and civic groups who had put up rewards for the capture of Officer Gullick's killer," I said. "Most of those won't pay off until he is convicted, but a few decided his arrest was close enough. I had a little bit to do with that, so they, um, well, I cashed a few checks. I have deducted my fee from that, so you don't owe me anything."

"Oh, my Lord," she said, quietly.

"And I kept a little more than your fee, to be honest and transparent, because I'm still trying to get Whiskey River Investigations to be a more steady gig, but . . ."

Amy was tearing up. "But what?"

I handed her the envelope. "There's a check in there, from me to you. I hope it helps."

She did not open the envelope. "Bless you."

"There will be more," I said.

She nodded and wiped away a tear. "Money will help. People have been very kind, but this is all going to be so expensive." Her chin quivered a bit. "I sold two of Donny's guitars." She sounded like she was telling a priest in confessional booth.

Donny finally spoke up. "Don't you worry about that, hon. Guitars are just wood and strings. Not real life."

I glanced at him. He was looking down at his shoes.

"I have something for you, too," I told him. I pulled another envelope from another pocket. This one was quite worn. I'd been carrying it a while. "It's the letter your wife asked me to give you. I realized I had not managed to do that. So, here it is."

Donny said nothing. Amy took the letter and handed it to her husband. He tucked it into his own jeans pocket, unread.

"Well," I said. "I'll let you all get back to family time and peanut butter. Take care."

"Bye!" Cassie ran in and gave me another hug. No snacks were ruined this time.

I headed to the door, but stopped when I heard Donny's voice. "Runyon?"

I turned to face him. "Yes, sir."

He glared at me, like I was a mythical beast. "You used to be a cop, right?"

"Yes, I did."

He stared at me for thirty seconds, as if that simple fact was the hardest thing in the world to process and comprehend.

"Well," he said. "Shit. I'll be damned."

ACKNOWLEDGMENTS

Can you believe this is the third Ed Runyon novel already?

I've spent countless hours here at my desk beneath the giant Godzilla poster my wife bought me, working on these books. The payoff is when someone like you decides to give the novel a chance. I appreciate it very much.

Ed Runyon has evolved since readers met him in *City Problems*. He is no longer a psychological mess. He's still stubborn, though, and impatient. I don't see that changing.

I'm not the only person who works on these books, though. My wife, Gere, and my friend Tom Williams read the books for me before I send them off to the publisher. They've done that for me through all four Spider John novels and now through every Ed Runyon book. Their advice and eagle-eye typo hunting are much appreciated.

Once I send the manuscript off to Bob and Pat Gussin at Oceanview Publishing, there is another whole team of people who work on the book, too. Pat provides spit and polish on any plot problems and reminds me I use the word "OK" too often. Then there are the art people who design the beautiful covers, the copy editors who chase down any typos still hiding in the manuscript, and the marketing people who get the word out to everyone. They are a great team.

I should not forget my agent, Evan Marshall, who helped me get into this novelist gig. Thanks, Evan.

And, of course, there is you, the person who brought this book home from the library or bought it at a neighborhood bookstore or online. Or maybe you borrowed it from a friend, or got it as a gift. It doesn't matter to me how you acquired it. Well, if you stole it, stop doing that. Bookstores have enough problems. But thanks for being a book person, reading for pleasure, leaving reviews or ratings, and seeking out new authors.

Book people are the best people.

BOOK CLUB
DISCUSSION QUESTIONS

1. If you had to classify *Go Find Daddy,* would you choose "hard-boiled detective fiction" or "small-town mystery thriller"?

2. What did you learn about rural Ohio, so-called "flyover" country? Different pace? Different attitudes? Different values? Different music? Anything that surprised you?

3. How do you relate to Ed Runyon as a human being? He's certainly not a superhero, but did you ever find yourself saying with admiration: "I could be Ed Runyon"?

4. This is the third Ed Runyon novel, and if you have read either *City Problems* or *Wayward Son,* were you able to detect any of the lingering depression that came with Ed to Ohio?

5. What is your opinion of the two women Ed is close to? Linda and Shelly?

6. Would you say that Ed is more of a "lone wolf" or a "team player"? Which works best for him?

7. How do you think the author handles "language" in this novel? With realism? Would you like more or fewer "cuss words"?

8. How do you think the volatile issue of "police misconduct" is handled? In a fair manner? Realistic manner?

9. Many of the characters in the Ed Runyon series have strong political and religious views. No matter your personal views, are you okay with this? Or do you think authors should avoid these polarizing issues in fiction?

10. Thinking of Ed Runyon's business, do you think he should move to a bigger city to give his fledgling PI business a chance? And thinking of Ed's future, what do you predict for him and Linda?

PUBLISHER'S NOTE

We trust that you enjoyed *Go Find Daddy*, the third in Steve Goble's
Ed Runyon Mystery Series.

While the other two novels stand on their own and can be read
in any order, the publication sequence is as follows:

CITY PROBLEMS
(Book 1)

A missing girl case sends Ed Runyon's life into
a dangerous downhill spiral. A moment of
violence—a snap judgment—Ed's life changes
to the core.

"Who would ever have thought that from the cornfields of Ohio a
fresh voice in crime fiction would emerge? In this debut outing of
a new series, Steve Goble delivers an authentic, compelling story of
a rural cop with a haunted past. *City Problems* is both a dynamic
procedural and an incisive portrait of a man at war with himself."

—WILLIAM KENT KRUEGER,
New York Times best-selling author

WAYWARD SON
(Book 2)

Ed Runyon goes hunting for a missing boy—
and ends up being prey.

"In *Wayward Son*, Steve Goble is unafraid to tackle the issues of our time head-on, but he does so in an elegant story filled with real, and fascinatingly flawed, characters." —MARK PRYOR, author

"Goble cranks up the heat in *Wayward Son*. It's a compelling page-turner with all the right moves." —RICK MOFINA, *USA Today* best-selling author

We hope that you will read the entire Ed Runyon Mystery Series and will look forward to more to come.

If you liked *Go Find Daddy*, we would be very appreciative if you would consider leaving a review. As you probably already know, book reviews are important to authors and they are very grateful when a reader makes the special effort to write a review, however brief.

For more information, please visit the author's website:
www.stevegoble.com.

Happy Reading,
Oceanview Publishing
Your Home for Mystery, Thriller, and Suspense